Halfhyde
at the Bight of Benin

Historical Fiction Published by McBooks Press

BY ALEXANDER KENT
Midshipman Bolitho
Stand Into Danger
In Gallant Company
Sloop of War
To Glory We Steer
Command a King's Ship
Passage to Mutiny
With All Despatch
Form Line of Battle!
Enemy in Sight!
The Flag Captain
Signal–Close Action!
The Inshore Squadron
A Tradition of Victory
Success to the Brave
Colours Aloft!
Honour This Day
The Only Victor
Beyond the Reef
The Darkening Sea
For My Country's Freedom
Cross of St George
Sword of Honour
Second to None
Relentless Pursuit
Man of War

BY DOUGLAS REEMAN
Badge of Glory
First to Land
The Horizon
Dust on the Sea
Twelve Seconds to Live
Battlecruiser
The White Guns

BY DAVID DONACHIE
The Devil's Own Luck
The Dying Trade
A Hanging Matter
An Element of Chance
The Scent of Betrayal
A Game of Bones

On a Making Tide
Tested by Fate

BY DUDLEY POPE
Ramage
Ramage & The Drumbeat
Ramage & The Freebooters
Governor Ramage R.N.
Ramage's Prize
Ramage & The Guillotine
Ramage's Diamond
Ramage's Mutiny
Ramage & The Rebels
The Ramage Touch
Ramage's Signal
Ramage & The Renegades
Ramage's Devil
Ramage's Trial
Ramage's Challenge
Ramage at Trafalgar
Ramage & The Saracens
Ramage & The Dido

BY C.N. PARKINSON
The Guernseyman
Devil to Pay
The Fireship
Touch and Go
So Near So Far
Dead Reckoning

BY V.A. STUART
Victors and Lords
The Sepoy Mutiny
Massacre at Cawnpore
The Cannons of Lucknow
The Heroic Garrison
The Valiant Sailors
The Brave Captains
Hazard's Command
Hazard of Huntress

BY R.F. DELDERFIELD
Too Few for Drums
Seven Men of Gascony

BY PHILIP MCCUTCHAN
Halfhyde at the Bight
of Benin
Halfhyde's Island

BY DEWEY LAMBDIN
The French Admiral
Jester's Fortune

BY JAN NEEDLE
A Fine Boy for Killing
The Wicked Trade
The Spithead Nymph

BY IRV C. ROGERS
Motoo Eetee

BY NICHOLAS NICASTRO
The Eighteenth Captain
Between Two Fires

BY FREDERICK MARRYAT
Frank Mildmay OR
The Naval Officer
The King's Own
Mr Midshipman Easy
Newton Forster OR
The Merchant Service
Snarleyyow OR
The Dog Fiend
The Privateersman
The Phantom Ship

BY W. CLARK RUSSELL
Wreck of the Grosvenor
Yarn of Old Harbour Town

BY RAFAEL SABATINI
Captain Blood

BY MICHAEL SCOTT
Tom Cringle's Log

BY A.D. HOWDEN SMITH
Porto Bello Gold

The Halfhyde Adventures, No. 1

Halfhyde at the Bight of Benin

Philip McCutchan

MCBOOKS PRESS, INC.
ITHACA, NEW YORK

Published by McBooks Press, Inc. 2004
Copyright © 1974 by Philip McCutchan
First published in the United Kingdom by A Barker, London,
as *Beware, Beware the Bight of Benin*

Cover painting: *River Class Destroyer at Speed* by Norman Wilkinson in
The Royal Navy, 1907. Courtesy of Mary Evans Picture Library.

Library of Congress Cataloging-in-Publication Data

McCutchan, Philip, 1920-
[Beware, Beware the Bight of Benin]
Halfhyde at the Bight of Benin / Philip McCutchan.
    p. cm. — (The Halfhyde adventures ; no. 1)
Originally published: Beware, Beware the Bight of Benin. London :
Barker, 1974.
    1. Halfhyde, St. Vincent (Fictitious character)—Fiction. 2. Great
Britain—History, Naval—Fiction. 3. Russians—Benin, Bight
of—Fiction. 4. Benin, Bight of—Fiction. I. Title.
    PR6063.A167B48 2004
    823'.914—dc22
                                                            2003022657

Distributed to the trade by National Book Network, Inc.,
15200 NBN Way, Blue Ridge Summit, PA 17214
800-462-6420

Additional copies of this book may be ordered from any bookstore or
directly from McBooks Press, Inc., ID Booth Building, 520 North Meadow
St., Ithaca, NY 14850. Please include $4.00 postage and
handling with mail orders. New York State residents must add
sales tax to total remittance (books & shipping). All McBooks Press
publications can also be ordered by calling toll-free
1-888-BOOKS11 (1-888-266-5711).
Please call to request a free catalog.

Visit the McBooks Press website at www.mcbooks.com.

Printed in the United States of America

9 8 7 6 5 4 3 2 1

Chapter 1

LIEUTENANT St Vincent Halfhyde, wakeful in the dank darkness of his tiny cabin, darkness slightly relieved by the dim
glow of a police light coming through the grating above his
door from the midshipmen's chest flat, listened to the many
sounds of the steel-sided 3000-ton cruiser, built in the late
1880s, as she rolled to a heavy beam-sea. All around there was
noise: from far below the thunder of shifting, storm-flung moun-
tains of coal in the bunkers; the drop and swill of ton upon
ton of water over the quarterdeck above his head; the creak of
hammock-clews against their rings as the off-watch midshipmen asleep outside in the flat swung to the roll; an overhead
rush of barefoot bluejackets and the wind-tossed shouts of petty
officers as a part of the watch was sent, clinging hard to the
lifelines, to secure the torn griping-bands of Number Five cutter, swaying from the davits below the after conning position;
the rythmic rattle of rifles against the chain running through
the trigger-guards as they stood in their racks, from farther aft
the stamp of the sentry provided by the Royal Marine Light
Infantry outside the cuddy; the thousand and one smaller noises
of any ship in a sea-way—the creak of woodwork, the roll of
personal gear left unsecured by careless snotties along the deck
of the chest flat, the eerie howl of wind in rigging, the boom-
ing slap of water along the armoured sides. Around all this, the

close, damp fug, the below-deck emanations of a ship battened-down for bad weather. It was a cold fug too: St Vincent Halfhyde cursed heartily, knowing that all too soon he would be much colder, knowing that in twenty minutes' time the bosun's pipes would be shrilling throughout the ship, along the mess decks and flats, to rouse the middle watch men. A fleeting thought: down below were six men who would never rouse again for a watch on deck; six corpses—one lieutenant, one gunner's mate, four seamen—already sewn into their canvas shrouds and currently lying in the cruiser's meat store, awaiting committal to the sea as soon as the weather should moderate. That, Halfhyde reflected, was the sea life: hardship, death, instant decision. After two years on half-pay, kicking his heels around London, an unemployed naval officer with little to support himself beyond that meagre half-pay, Halfhyde was glad enough to feel again the lift of a deck beneath him. Yet there were moments when he hated the sea with an intensity that racked his mind and body, and left him shocked, shaken by the fury that was in him.

Only four days earlier, Halfhyde, in his lodgings in Camden Town, had received a telegram from the Admiralty: he was to report in uniform to the office of the Second Sea Lord, at eleven am that very forenoon. In a fever of excitement, but also with some trepidation, Halfhyde had foraged for his long laid aside uniform in its metal cases on the top of the vast wardrobe that almost filled his bedroom. He had shaved carefully, dressed with nervously shaking fingers. The uniform fitted still: there was a sharp smell of mothballs, but otherwise he was a naval officer once again. He looked at his reflection in a long looking-glass. Carefully, he brushed the frock-coat with its two gold rings on either cuff, pulled down the starched shirt-cuffs until the dark blue cloth of the frock-coat tightened around them, seeming starched itself. Thus clad, he went to his sitting-room for breakfast.

The sight of him startled Mrs Mavitty, his landlady. She stood staring, arms raised in wonder.

"Lawks, sir, what's come over you?"

Halfhyde smiled, softening the hard lines of a long face. "The telegram, Mrs Mavitty."

"Oh, dearie me, sir, there's never going to be a war, is there?"

"I doubt it, Mrs Mavitty, I doubt it." He sat, pulling up his trouser-legs, resting his elbows on the table, where stood coffee, a heated dish of kedgeree, toast and marmalade. Almost guiltily, he stole a look at the stripes of gold lace with the executive curl above. "It's no compliment, Mrs Mavitty, to suggest that it would take a war to persuade Their Lordships to . . . take an interest in me."

"Their Lordships, Mr Halfhyde?"

"The Board of Admiralty, Mrs Mavitty. It's possible I may be leaving you." Halfhyde could not check the rising hope in his voice. The last two years had been comfortable in a sense, for Mrs Mavitty was kindness itself, and her terms for a steadily paying gentleman were moderate. But half-pay was no bed of roses for an active man, whose profession of Her Majesty's Service—for such it had remained—precluded his participation in any lesser occupations. "In the meantime, my good woman, you have forgotten the hot milk."

"The hot milk, sir?" Mrs Mavitty seemed overcome at the sight of her lodger in his naval splendour. "Dearie me, sir, I'll forget me own head next," and she went off as fast as her bulk could carry her, and could be heard shouting for Mavitty her husband, in tones she would never have employed for Mr Halfhyde.

Halfhyde that morning ate with little appetite, absently. After his breakfast he sat looking out of his window, down into the tawdry streets of Camden Town, and the dust, and the horse manure, and the busy carts, the men and women moving about their affairs in workaday London, not seeing them, but seeing instead more nostalgic and more wondrous things from his own past: the splendid sight of a British Battle Squadron at sea in line ahead, the strings of coloured bunting blowing out from the signal halliards, or the winking masthead lights at night; a great concourse of seaworn grey ships entering Malta's Grand Harbour to anchor together on the signal from the flagship, the lower- and quarter-booms being swung out, the boats and gang-ways lowered, and the anchors let go at split-second timing, all together, as the engines thrashed astern to bring the ships up; misty dawns in Scottish anchorage, with a red sun behind the haze rose-tinting the distant, towering hills as the White Ensign was hoisted to the jackstaff to the strains of martial music, the bugles echoing, savage and triumphant, as they blared out for Colours; a steam picket-boat coming alongside a cruiser's quarterdeck ladder, her crew soaked in the spray of a brisk morning; the Northern Lights, viewed from a torpedo-boat's bridge off Lyness, or the Old Man of Hoy standing out to starboard, in broad daylight even at two bells in the middle watch, as a ship steamed north about through the Pentlands from the Firth of Forth to the Clyde; the wondrous, fairy like beauty of Kyle of Lochalsh and a night passage under moonlight of the Minch with the Isle of Skye to port and a wind coming through the Sound of Harris; a cruiser battling through boisterous seas in the Great Australian Bight with a roaring gale blowing straight off the southern ice; China-side, and the mysteries and glamour of the East, and dances on the quarterdeck beneath the awnings in Trincomalee and Singapore. And other things too, less pleasant things, but all part and parcel of the same life: wars, and death, and vindictive senior officers who believed that their powers were derived from God Himself.

But very different from Camden Town, and half-pay.

At 10:15, Lieutenant St Vincent Halfhyde called down to Mrs Mavitty: "A cab, if you please. Will you be good enough to send Mavitty?"

"That I will, sir." The shouts for Mavitty were renewed, boisterously. Within five minutes Halfhyde was on his way, his sword dangling between his knees from the gilded sword-belt round his waist.

"Captain, this is Mr Halfhyde. Mr Halfhyde—Captain Fitzsimmons."

Halfhyde slightly inclined his head, heels together. Captain Fitzsimmons extended a hand. The grip was hard. Halfhyde looked into the eyes of Captain the Honourable Quentin Fitzsimmons and knew he looked into the eyes of a hard man, an officer known throughout the Service for two things in particular: a ruthless dedication to duty which had made him a fine, if cautious, seaman, and a terrible liking for the aristocracy. Captain Fitzsimmons, an aristocrat himself, could naturally not be accused of snobbishness, but it was whispered in the Fleet that his prediction for gently born officers verged at times upon undermining his undoubted devotion to strict duty. For example, Captain Fitzsimmons never unbent to his engineer officers. They were not, and by their calling could not be, gentlemen, let alone in any way connected with the aristocracy, so Captain Fitzsimmons never spoke to them other than officially. All this Halfhyde knew, and as a result was much puzzled, for he had put two and two together and had failed to find a suitable answer. He was, he felt strongly, being introduced to his new Commanding Officer, but he was well aware that he was no aristocrat. His father, a prosperous enough farmer in the Yorkshire Dales, had contributed to his training in HMS *Britannia* but by no means to his likely inclusion in the favour of Captain Fitzsimmons.

Halfhyde looked at the officer in whose mahogany-darkened Admiralty office this meeting was taking place, a portly rear-admiral, white-haired, red-faced, and very short of breath. The brass buttons of his frock coat, Halfhyde saw, were as strained as the bowels of a constipated bitch. Halfhyde's look was an enquiring one, and it was answered by the Rear-Admiral.

"Captain Fitzsimmons commands the *Aurora*, presently lying at Portsmouth," the Rear-Admiral puffed at him. "You are being offered an appointment as a lieutenant under his command."

Halfhyde fought down rising excitement, managed to keep his face austere and non-committal. "And Captain Fitzsimmons?" he asked deferentially. "I take it he is . . . agreeable?"

Fitzsimmons, a tall man, heavily bearded, very thin, nodded. "No objections," he said. He failed, however, to sound keen. St Vincent Halfhyde conjectured that already he would have been looked up, fruitlessly, in Burke's Landed Gentry. A look passed between Fitzsimmons and the Rear-Admiral. The latter gave a cough, and spoke to Halfhyde.

"Captain Fitzsimmons," he said portentously, "has been *informed*. He is fully *aware*."

"Of my record, sir, as officially written down?"

Stiffly, the Rear-Admiral nodded. "Two years on half-pay, following upon a . . . disagreement with your Captain."

"A disagreement that was none of my making, sir, as well you must know—"

"Mr Halfhyde—"

"And you must also know that an enquiry was refused me—"

"Mr Halfhyde, do you wish to talk yourself out of an appointment? For damme, sir, you are close upon doing so!" The Rear-Admiral, redder in the face than ever, huffed and puffed alarmingly. "The past is the past, Mr Halfhyde, and only a foolish man would attempt to disturb it now. Captain Fitzsimmons is prepared to overlook such matters in the interest of—of Admiralty requirements. This is your chance, Mr Halfhyde. Accept this appointment, and you will go back on the full-pay list as of the moment you do so."

"And the appointment, sir? Its nature, if I may ask?"

"You will be appointed as a watchkeeping lieutenant of less than eight years seniority to Her Majesty's cruiser *Aurora*, vice Mr Lewis—"

"And Mr Lewis?"

"Was lost overboard in a sea-way off Finisterre, whilst *Aurora* was homeward bound from Gibraltar. Do you not read the papers, Mr Halfhyde?"

Halfhyde gave a wintry smile. "On half-pay, sir?"

"There is no occasion for jocularity," the Rear-Admiral snapped.

"No more there is in the predicament of half-pay," Halfhyde said. In fact he recalled a column in the *Morning Post* some weeks earlier. Mr Lewis had indeed gone overboard in full view of one, apparently helpless, witness; the incident had been noted in the deck and fair-copy logs, and that was all. A man had died and a frugal Treasury had been graciously spared the expense of a naval funeral ashore. Halfhyde turned to his new Captain. "I accept the appointment gratefully, sir."

Fitzsimmons nodded, his face expressionless. "There are other aspects," he said. "You should know about these, and Rear-Admiral Masters will confirm a degree of secrecy in what I have to say . . ."

Halfhyde was ordered to join his ship next day. That evening he visited his club for the first time in two years. He had kept up his subscription, but actual attendance was beyond his means, for he was a man who preferred not to indulge himself at all unless he could indulge to the full. That night he celebrated with friends of whom also he had not seen much during his two years on half-pay, and had a decent skinful of drink, after which he repaired to the room of a lady friend known on the stage as Tiny Teazer.

In the morning, after a leavetaking, tearful on her part, he went back by hansom cab to Camden Town; paid his last bill; said good-bye to the Mavittys, who were sad to see him go; and, in frock-coat, cap, and sword, went to Waterloo station, for Portsmouth Town, with all his gear. Making for a first-class carriage, he saw ahead of him, also about to enter the train with a nicely-dressed, veiled lady bidding him good-bye, a small uni-formed, midshipman, a species more familiarly known throughout the British Navy simply as a wart.

Feeling the need for naval company however lowly, Halfhyde moved on, saluted the veiled lady, who smiled back somewhat warily upon seeing his uniform, and joined the Portsmouth-bound wart, who in point of fact looked thoroughly embarrassed at being caught with his mother by a high and mighty lieu-tenant. The wart, still on the platform, almost tore himself in two with a smart salute. Halfhyde was regretfully conscious that he had spoiled the fond farewell: a kiss was frantically dodged just before the guard's whistle blew, and the wart embarked.

The train began to pull out, and mother fell behind. The wart looked at Halfhyde. Halfhyde smiled. "For God's sake," he said, "wave! Dammit, she's your mother!"

"Oh! Thank you, sir!" The small wart leapt up, flung him-self at the window, hung out and waved. Halfhyde grinned. He remembered his own wart days well enough: his tearful mother; his father being very withdrawn and proud but obviously wish-ing young St Vincent had stayed to help on the slopes of the Wensleydale fells; the bullying in the gunrooms of the Fleet; the harsh discipline; the fearsome arrogance of some lieutenants of over eight years seniority—that line of demarcation which, having once been passed, entitled the lieutenant to a gold half-stripe between the two full ones, and much increase in pay; the bloody-mindedness of Commanders when warts made more juvenile noise then they were entitled to stun their seniors' ears with. Of course there had been the compensations: the thrill of a first command—command of the Duty Steam Picket Boat, the link between ships of a squadron at anchor, when a wart had to show himself both a seaman and an officer able to command coxswain and crew, each old enough to be his father and with enough collective sea-time behind them to reach back almost to the days of Nelson; the awed adoration of young women, who liked to dance with a brassbound bum-freezer jacket; the company of real men rather than the clerkly popinjays of civil life—real men who nine times out of ten were decent men also, behind the snap and golden glitter of sea-going autocracy. Yes, they had been good days . . .

Smiling at the wart, Halfhyde threw a conversational ball as the train gathered speed in its cloud of smoke and steam. "What ship?"

"*Aurora,* sir."

Halfhyde laughed. "Well, I'll be damned! So am I. Your first ship—as a wart, I mean?"

"Yes, sir."

"Name?"

"Runcorn, sir."

"Runcorn? H'm—familiar, that. Trafalgar."

"Yes, sir."

"A forebear?"

The wart nodded vigorously, looking proud and pleased. "A great-uncle of my father's, sir. He was a midshipman under Admiral Nelson."

"I'm sure you're proud," Halfhyde said, and added, "as I am of mine. I, too, had an ancestor at Trafalgar."

"Really, sir? Who, sir?"

"Daniel Halfhyde . . . gunner's mate in the *Temeraire.*"

There was an amused look in Halfhyde's eye at the wart's reaction, which was one of embarrassment. It was a quirk of St

Vincent Halfhyde's character to enjoy such reactions when he thus revealed his humble but gallant forebear's lower-deck status. The wart was speechless and Halfhyde began to feel sorry: his audience was too young, too set into the *Britannia's* mould, and probably thought the lieutenant guilty of tactlessness. Halfhyde laughed and said, "Our Captain will be delighted with you—you've scored a point of favour even before you've set foot aboard, my lad!"

"Really, sir?"

Halfhyde said no more about that. It could smack of disloyalty, and Halfhyde was not a disloyal officer, though he could be an outspoken and even a disobedient one. His feuds with senior officers had always been conducted in the open, without intrigue. But he knew he had said no more than the truth. Halfhyde knew his naval history: the Runcorn who had sailed with Nelson, and who had subsequently died whilst still a midshipman from a fever caught in Egypt, had been one Lord Charles Runcorn, an aristocrat if ever there was one—as possibly Captain Fitzsimmons, in confirming this wart's appointment to his command, had already known.

At Portsmouth there was high excitement that morning. It was 28 February 1891, an auspicious occasion: Her Majesty Queen Victoria, making one of her now rare appearances in public, was to launch two ships for the enhancement of the British Fleet—the first-class cruiser *Royal Arthur,* to be of 7700 tons displacement when fitted out, and a splendid battleship of 14,150 tons, the *Royal Sovereign.* As a result Portsmouth was in festive mood. Looking down from the High Level platform into the square where the magnificent Town Hall had been but recently completed, Halfhyde and his attendant wart had seen a military band playing, and armed companies of soldiers marching past the Mayor and Corporation and high-ranking naval and military officers, to head beneath the High Level itself and on past Aggie Weston's teetotal Royal Sailors Rest, to turn into Edinburgh Road for the Unicorn Gate into the dockyard. A large crowd, virtuously thanking God for fine weather, cheered and waved Union Flags. Distantly in the dockyard could be seen the yards and mastheads and fighting-tops of the great grey-painted steel warships, dressed overall with coloured bunting in honour of the Queen. Halfhyde clutching his gilded sword, felt quite a lump in his throat as he listened to the resounding brass of the Royal Inniskilling Fusiliers. After his period in the wilderness, he was part of this scene once again, and if he behaved himself, the Rear-Admiral had said, might remain so. Remembering this, Halfhyde's lip curled a little: he disliked being talked to like a child. Thinking of children—for Mr Midshipman Runcorn at fifteen was little more—Halfhyde turned to the waiting wart.

"We'll not arrive aboard together," he said kindly. Gunrooms did not take well to favouritism from the wardroom, and a first arrival in company could easily enough be misconstrued, even if only intentionally. "Here's a porter," he added, as an elderly greybeard in the calico-sleeved waistcoat of the London and South-Western Railway Company hove in sight with a barrow. "Let him call you a cab. As for me, I've somewhere to go first."

The wart saluted, met his eye squarely. He knew the ropes after his time as a naval cadet in the *Britannia* and the Training Squadron. This chance meeting in the train was, like Halfhyde's own experiences, now in the past. The ship-future loomed, daunting but inevitable, and there would be no attempt to curry favour with lieutenants. Leaving the wart looking somewhat desolate nevertheless—for in a sense the exalted officer had been a link with mother—Halfhyde strode down the platform, waylaid the oncoming porter and barrow, told him to get out his gear and keep an eye on it until his return, and went down the steps clutching his sword. The old porter meandered towards the guard's van and did his work; the train, the last one through from Waterloo before Her Majesty's, the royal coaches of which would be by-passed on to the branch line into the dockyard, pulled out of the station in a cloud of smoke and steam. Its disembarked passengers milled about Mr Runcorn, who found himself submerged in a draft of blue jackets sweating into serge uniforms as, under a bearded and swearing petty officer, they humped up bags and hammocks for the march through the streets of Portsmouth to the barrack-hulks in the dockyard.

Lieutenant Halfhyde proceeded to an hotel close to the railway station, where, in the lounge, he sent a waiter scurrying for whisky. While he waited, he ruminated on the somewhat strange circumstances surrounding his unexpected appointment.

Queen Street, along which Mr Runcorn passed on his quaking way to the dockyard, was every stone a sailor's thoroughfare. Along it, generations of British seamen had walked or staggered, drunk or whored their hilarious, shanty or bawdy song singing way to and from the wooden walls, then the iron walls, and now the steel walls, of England. Much beer and gin had flowed, also a modicum of blood, for sailors ashore tended to fight as they did at sea. The constables of the law had a hard time of it when a fleet was in port, but, being tolerant or perhaps merely wise men, they largely turned a blind eye and concentrated on the paltry civilian population. Pompey, not just Queen Street, was a sailor's town: at any given moment there would be upwards of ten thousand bluejackets and marines from the ships and the barrack-hulks and the training establishments, men fresh from home or just come back from Malta, Chinaside, the West Indies, South Africa . . . from wherever the flag of empire floated in the splendid name of Her Majesty Queen Victoria. Mr Runcorn, wart, green as grass, looked out on Queen Street as the four-wheeler drew him inexorably towards his destiny. Already the street was thronged with sailors—libertymen from the fleet, off-duty watchkeepers, seamen, stokers, signalmen—or with messmen going about their purchasing duties for the various messes of the ships: Captain's galley, wardroom, gunroom, warrant officers' mess, chief and petty officers' mess. And already, despite the good intentions of Aggie Weston, a good deal of beer had flowed: some of the bluejackets rolled and sang songs undeniably offensive, had she heard them, to Her Majesty, sitting in her ornately furnished drawing-room coach somewhere between Windsor Castle and Pompey Town. It was all part of Portsmouth. Bars and brothels and bawdy songs were inextricably linked with the men who manned the fleet, just as much as was "Rule, Britannia" that would that day be beaten out by the brass of the military band as the great ships of war moved down the slipways.

Mr Runcorn's arrival at the South Railway jetty, where the *Aurora* was berthed, was lacking in the dignity due to be accorded Lieutenant Halfhyde's. Once past the constable of the dockyard police, who saluted smartly and enquired the four-wheeler's destination, polite consideration vanished. The carriage, rumbling over cobbles, past figureheads of old ships from the sailing navy, past the boatyard with its sea smells of tar and rope and canvas, turned left beneath a stone arch and stopped beside the quarterdeck ladder of a long grey cruiser, from whose two funnels trails of smoke were already rising. As Mr Runcorn disembarked, he was met by a shout from a frock-coated lieutenant bearing his two gold stripes importantly and wearing an empty sword-belt in indication of his current status as Officer of the Watch. A telescope with gleaming brasswork was pointed like a hostile gun at Mr Runcorn.

"You there. *That wart.*"

Runcorn saluted smartly. "Sir?" he piped.

"Get that damn contraption out of it, and remove your obnoxious self at the same time. Captain's going ashore."

The terrified wart froze: it was too late for movement, for a sudden scurry of offensiveness out of the path of God—God was already manifesting. As the side party fell in at the head of the ladder, a cap was seen to rise from a hatchway guarded by polished brass stanchions threaded with pipe-clayed rope ending in massive turk's-heads. The emerging deity, gold-haloed around the peak of his cap, wearing four gold rings on either cuff of his frock coat, stepped on to the deck and stalked to the side. There were salutes, and the thin, rising and falling wail of the bosun's pipe. The Captain, without a word to the Officer of the Watch, came down the ladder and set a highly-polished foot on the stonework of the jetty. Mr Runcorn saluted. The Captain returned the salute gravely, and stopped.

"Mr Runcorn, I presume?"

"Y-y-yessir."

"Voice not broken yet. Something needs to drop."

The wart went a very deep red. The Captain went on, "Ancestor at Trafalger, under Nelson, what?"

"Y-y-yessir."

"There's hope for you, then." The Captain turned away and strode off beneath the arch, wrapping a boat-cloak around his angular body against a keen breeze sweeping into the harbour past Fort Blockhouse. The wart saluted the turned back, looked up appealingly at the Officer of the Watch, and was admitted aboard.

Chapter 2

HALFHYDE, reporting aboard after the Captain's departure to the office of the Commander-in-Chief, Portsmouth, was shown to the wardroom by a side-boy detached from the gangway staff by the Corporal of the Gangway, a Royal Marine Artilleryman. In the wardroom, Halfhyde was greeted by another officer of lieutenant's rank, who introduced himself as Cotterrell.

"Replacing poor Lewis?" Cotterrell asked.

"That's right. I'm sorry. I'm sure he's a loss."

Cotterrell said, "That's true. He was a good fellow, but that's the Service, when all's said and done. Care for a drink? Bar's open."

"Whisky," Halfhyde said absently. "A quick one. Then I'll be around the ship. I understand we sail at two bells?"

"Right," Cotterrell said. He beckoned the Marine servant and ordered one whisky, one gin. "For the Gulf of Guinea," he said when the servant had departed. "Or more precisely, the Bight of Benin."

"You know that?" Halfhyde asked.

"Why not? Nothing secret about it, is there?" The officer stared curiously at Halfhyde.

Halfhyde shrugged off-handedly. "Not for me to say. I don't suppose there is. Have you been there before?"

"No. We've been in the Mediterranean till we came back for

dry-docking. Before that I was in river gunboats. China-side."
He paused. "You?"

"Oh, I've done my time on the coast," Halfhyde said non-
committally. The drinks came. Halfhyde reached out for his,
drank the whisky down in one swallow, and stood up. "Thank
you, that was kind of you. I'll return the compliment later." He
stalked out of the wardroom, leaving Cotterrell to gape at apparent incivility. Halfhyde, in Cotterrell's view, looked like being a
queer fellow. For his part, Halfhyde was itching to walk the
decks of a man-of-war again, to soak himself in the age-old
smells of tar and rope and the newer ones of machinery. He
went out on the upper deck and turned forward, going up the
ladder from the quarterdeck to the after conning position, and
on forward past the funnels in their skylighted casing towards
the navigating bridge and flag deck. The Bight of Benin—which
destination happened to be one of the reasons for the Admiralty's choice of Halfhyde, since he had some specialized
knowledge of those difficult waters—could wait: he was renew-
ing acquaintance with an old friend, a seagoing vessel of war.
From the navigating bridge, where a seaman was polishing the
brass of the binnacle, Halfhyde looked down on the great six-
inch muzzle-loading guns behind the fo'c'sle. They might well
be used, though the *Aurora's* mission was to prevent the out-
break of war rather than bring it about. Halfhyde reflected.
Unlike his lowly ancestor of Trafalgar, he was no gunnery man,
but he knew muzzle-loaders to be outdated. For some years
now the British Navy had used breech-loaders, reverting to earlier ideas. The muzzle-loaders, which had their limitations and
their dangers in comparison with breech-loaders, had proved a
flash in the pan, but in ship-construction flashes in pans tended

to linger embarrassingly as monuments to rashness. Halfhyde's point of aim changed.

Behind him on the flag deck, a yeoman of signals, a small, thin man with the face of an anxious monkey, was busy with a telescope. Halfhyde looked in the same direction. The yeoman was reading off a string of flags hoisted to the starboard fore upper yard of an incoming battleship, the flagship of the Channel Fleet. The First Battle Squadron was leading in a line of grey, sea-worn battleships and cruisers, monsters moving slowly past Fort Blockhouse.

Once again, Halfhyde felt a lump in his throat. He had been away too long, too long.

Just aft of the yeoman, a leading-signalman was using mechanical semaphore arms in an extraordinary rapid exchange with the flag deck of another ship, HMS *Marathon,* a cruiser of a class some years more advanced than *Aurora.* All movement of ferries between Portsmouth Hard and Gosport had been suspended for the stately entry of the Channel Fleet. Halfhyde watched, standing motionless as the great battleships moved past, exchanging bugle salutes with the *Aurora* and with other warships. Men were fallen in along their decks, long lines of seamen in sennet hats and clean blue collars, men who would soon be fallen out for the operation of anchoring, swinging out boats and booms, or of going alongside the various shoreside berths. The flagship proceeded up harbour, vanishing beyond the rest of the battle squadron. Halfhyde guessed she would turn in the wider reaches and then in due course come down to take over the South Railway jetty when the *Aurora* cleared away to sea. Admirals liked the South Railway jetty: it was closer to the dockyard's main gate. Halfhyde watched the entry of the smaller craft, the gunboats, sloops and torpedo-boats, with professional interest, then went below decks.

He was making his way past the open door of the gunroom when he heard the swish, swish of a cane. In the lee of some ventilator shafting, he stopped and looked. He frowned. The wart of the Portsmouth train was bent over the back of a chair, the seat of his best Number One trousers strained and shiny across his backside. Behind him, a short, fat sub-lieutenant was bringing a cane down hard.

Six of the best—it was by no means unusual, and the sub of the gunroom had the authority. But for a newly joined wart? What in heaven's name could the boy have done already?

Halfhyde shrugged. That authority of the sub's was fairly absolute: he had virtually total power over the lives of the midshipmen. Few Executive Officers would interfere with those powers, the Captain never. In the Royal Navy iron discipline was the order of the day and to undermine it was unthinkable. St Vincent Halfhyde moved on, his face hard. Bullying was not discipline and he hated it, but dare not show favouritism lest the bullying increase. Moving away, he shrugged again, and grinned faintly. The boy would have to knuckle under as others had done before him; and in time it would stop. Warts, after all, were warts.

"Now shout it," the sub of the gunroom said when the punishment was over. "*What is a midshipman?* Come along, Mr Runcorn, loud and clear."

Mr Runcorn, trembling, filled his lungs, rubbed at his stinging rump, and obeyed orders. Loudly he answered: "A midshipman is the lowest form of animal life in the Royal Navy."

"Sir."

"Sir, sir."

"And now again—louder. *Much* louder." The Sub-Lieutenant swung the cane suggestively. "Come, Mr Runcorn, you are shouting it into a full gale of wind and you wish to be heard."

"MIDSHIPMEN," bawled Mr Runcorn, "ARE THE LOWEST FORM OF ANIMAL LIFE IN THE ROYAL NAVY."

At noon the hands were piped to dinner by the busy bosun's mates, and representatives of each broadside mess mustered to draw their watered rum. In the gunroom the midshipmen sat down to luncheon. The dinner hour, however, was not a time of repose for Mr Runcorn. The Commander, Executive Officer of the cruiser, found this a convenient moment to speak to the newly joined wart. A seaman boy knocked on the gunroom door and entered, removing his headgear as he did so, placing it beneath his left arm and standing rigidly at attention.

"Mr Runcorn, sir?"

"Yes?"

Mr Runcorn failed to notice the look on the face of the sub of the gunroom; so did the seaman boy, who advanced into the small compartment which was almost filled by the table and by the worn leather settee that ran the full length, below a line of highly polished brass ports. The boy approached the midshipman and bent to speak.

"You," the sub roared.

The boy started, stared. "Sir?"

"And you, Mr Runcorn!"

"Yes, sir?"

"Yes, *sub,* in here, when strictly off duty. Not sir. That's fault number two. Number one: you do not receive messages behind the backs of your superiors." He pointed a finger at the trembling seaman boy. "You, wretched boy, should first have asked my permission, as Mess President, to speak to Mr Runcorn. Do you not understand the way gentlemen live?"

"N-no, sir. I—"

"Hold your tongue. Who sent you?"

"Commander, sir."

"I see. Then you may speak to Mr Runcorn. I take it the Commander wishes to see Mr Runcorn, and Mr Runcorn may go. When Mr Runcorn comes back, he will prepare for another six of the best. Mr Runcorn, go."

Runcorn went, with a beating heart, thinking thoughts of home. He followed the messenger along a maze of steel-lined alleyways, past overall-clad working-parties busy through the dinner hour on last-minute preparations for sea, up and down ladders, in and out of hatches, until the seaman boy halted outside a door, one of many in another alleyway inside the midship superstructure. The boy knocked and went in.

"Commander, sir. Mr Runcorn, sir." He stepped back, and the wart entered. The cabin was small, the bunk, wash-hand-basin and wardrobe leaving little enough room for the desk behind which sat Commander Gordon.

The Commander waved a hand. "Sit down, snotty."

"Thank you, sir." The wart hesitated. "Er . . . may I stand, please, sir?" His rump was sore and stinging. At lunch, the sub had not allowed him to stand and the soreness had become worse. The thought of another beating was sheer torture.

The Commander's eyes narrowed. "What's the matter?"

"Nothing, sir."

"Nothing? H'm. Taken six of the best, I suppose." Suddenly the Commander caught the glint of tears. "Steady on, man! You're not going to blub, surely to God? A midshipman blubbing? Dammit, you're no longer a blasted cadet!"

"No, sir." The shivering wart took a grip. "I'm sorry, sir."

The Commander grunted, looking at the white face closely still. "Very well, Mr Runcorn, you may stand." He paused. "This is your first ship as a snotty, right?"

"Yes, sir."

"You'll find she's a happy one, though you don't look as though you think so at the moment. Taut but happy. You'll have heard the saying, taut ships make happy ships, and happy ships make efficient ships?"

"Yes, sir."

"Help to keep it that way, then." The Commander smiled. He had a very ready smile, and he seemed friendly. "Promptness, attentiveness to duty, clear speech so everyone knows what order you've given or what report you've made, alertness at all times. Above all, perhaps, *willingness* at all times. You'll find senior officers who'll demand the impossible when you're tired, wet, and bloody miserable. When they do, a cheerful manner and an alert response go a long way, and are remembered when the conduct reports go in later. Bear it in mind, Mr Runcorn."

"Aye, aye, sir."

"That's all, then. And I'm glad to have you aboard. Off you go."

"Aye, aye, sir." Mr Runcorn turned about and took the one step necessary to reach the door. He was outside, pondering on the strangeness of being so punctiliously addressed as "Mister" by his seniors, when he was called back.

"Wart!"

Mr Runcorn went back in. "Rubbing's the worse thing possible," the Commander said with a grin. "I speak from experience long ago!"

Lieutenant Halfhyde was sent for when Captain Fitzsimmons returned from shore. "Our conversation in the Admiralty," the Captain said, bidding him sit. "You know the orders."

"Yes, sir."

"Would you care for sherry, Mr Halfhyde?" The offer was made without warmth.

Halfhyde shook his head. "Thank you, sir, no."

Captain Fitzsimmons looked up at his servant, who was hovering expectantly. "One glass," he said. "Then get out."

"Aye, aye, sir." There was silence while sherry was brought for the Captain, who spent the interval looking gloomily out of a scuttle towards Gosport. When the servant had gone he turned again to Halfhyde. "I sent for you so as to clear the air," he said slowly. "You know, and I know, that there are two reasons for your appointment to my ship, and two only: your knowledge of the Russian language and the Russian Navy, and your navigational experience in the Gulf of Guinea. This is understood, Mr Halfhyde?"

"It is, sir. May I ask why you stress it?"

The Captain stared bleakly, pulling at his beard. "Yes, you may. I stress it because I would not otherwise have allowed myself to be the instrument by which you have been brought back from the half-pay list, Mr Halfhyde. I have no time for officers who come into dispute with their captains."

"Sir, I—"

"And had I been the captain concerned, I would have had you court martialled without—"

"When you would, I think, have had the verdict go against you. In any event, as it was, Lord Cleveland was not inclined to put it to the test. As for my own attempts to secure an enquiry—"

"Have a care, Mr Halfhyde!" Fitzsimmons had risen and was standing behind a chair, hands resting on its back, staring at Halfhyde. He made a formidable figure, one very conscious of the immense powers of the captain of a ship of war. "There is to be no dispute with me, no repetition of the past—"

"For you will be watching every move I make," Halfhyde broke in, his colour high on the cheekbones of a long, somewhat sallow face, and his lips faintly curling with disdain. He got to his feet, formidable himself, and furiously angry, with a strong sense of unfairness. "Sir, I shall do my best under your command to carry out the express orders of the Board of Admiralty. I hope, as they do, that a state of war with Russia can be avoided—my efforts will be directed that way, I assure you. But once I am successful, sir, I shall no longer feel in need of your patronage. The Admiralty will see that I am properly and fully employed. Is *that* understood?"

"You—you—"

"And now, sir, with your permission, I shall carry on." Without waiting for formal permission to do so, Halfhyde turned away and left the cuddy.

•   •   •

Climbing to the navigating bridge a little before two bells in the afternoon watch, by which time the orders had been passed to single-up the ropes to the jetty, Captain Fitzsimmons was clearly in a furious temper—the jut of his gingerish beard customarily acted as a weathervane to his subordinates. The Captain, glancing with a seaman's eye at tide, wind, and surface, registered a promise of continuing fair weather; the sky was powder-blue, with some small clumps of cirro-cumulus to seaward. Tall, majestic, carrying a telescope, the Captain stalked into the starboard wing and glared down at the narrow space of water where the ship's side was held off the wall by catamarans placed fore and aft. Then he swung round on his assembled bridge staff: the navigating officer—a senior lieutenant whose station for leaving harbour was that of Officer of the Watch, a midshipman, a yeoman of signals, a leading-signalman, a quartermaster, two lookouts and two seamen boys, the latter to act as messengers. The Captain addressed the navigating officer.

"Mr Richards."

"Sir?"

"My compliments to Mr Halfhyde." Fitzsimmons pulled at his beard. "He is to report to the bridge." He turned away and waited as a messenger was sent aft at the double. Down on the jetty the rope-handling parties awaited their further unberthing orders; across the dockyard great cranes were busy; and in the stream there was a hooting of steam-whistles as the small harbour craft scurried for shelter on the orders of the Queen's Harbour Master to clear the way for the outward passage of one of Her Majesty's ships of war, bound on her great occasions across the world. The Captain stared broodingly at Gosport and

Fort Blockhouse, and up the long harbour towards the fortress-capped Portsdown Hill to the east of the old castle at Porchester.

Halfhyde came up and saluted.

"Ah, Mr Halfhyde." A pause. "Mr Halfhyde, I wish to see whether or no you have lost your touch."

Halfhyde stared, eyes wide. "I beg your pardon, sir?"

"You will take the ship off the jetty and out to sea. You have two minutes in which to study the chart." Fitzsimmons called again to the navigating officer: "Mr Richards, you will allow Mr Halfhyde a sight of your chart for the port approaches and Spithead."

"Aye, aye, sir." Richards indicated his chart, laid out on a projecting shelf in the after part of the navigating bridge. Halfhyde went over and studied the soundings, buoys and leading-marks. Within the specified two minutes, he looked up. "I shall have no further use for the chart, sir," he said coolly.

"You must have an excellent memory, Mr Halfhyde."

"I have, sir, I have." Halfhyde turned to the navigator. "Mr Richards, since I am to act in the room of the Captain, may I be told when tugs will arrive?"

"The Captain," Richards said quietly, "doesn't use tugs."

Halfhyde nodded. "I see. In that case, neither shall I. I shall want the port bower anchor veered to the waterline. Will you please give the order?"

Richards nodded and passed the order to the cable party on the fo'c'sle. Halfhyde walked into the wing, joining the Captain. He turned to study the incoming tide, now almost at the flood but still with some thrust left in it. He said, "I shall come off on the tide, using the spring as a pivot."

There was no response from the Captain, who nevertheless

watched closely. Halfhyde gave his orders in a calm, brisk voice: "Let go headrope, sternrope and backspring. Stand by main engines."

The ropes came off. Halfhyde looked down at the water, his face expressionless. There was little movement of the ship off the wall as yet: the tide was not quite strong enough after all to take her. The engines would have to give her a nudge. Halfhyde turned. "Main engines slow ahead." Within half a minute there was a rumble from below, a belch of thick black smoke from the after funnel, and the ship began to shake throughout her length as the action of the screw pushed her ahead against the retaining influence of the spring, the last remaining rope that led from the starboard bitts on the fo'c'sle head, through the bull-ring in the eyes of the ship, to the set of bollards on the jetty level with the break of the after super-structure. Under the power of her engines, the *Aurora* swung her stern out across the harbour, and Halfhyde passed the last orders for leaving England: "Let go spring, slow astern main engines. Port twenty. Stop main engines, wheel amidships. Half ahead main engines . . . starboard ten . . . midships. Steady." He turned to the Captain. "Sir, I have not, I think, lost my touch."

The two men's eyes met and held. It was the Captain who looked away first.

Pointing for the harbour entrance, HM cruiser *Aurora* made for the open sea. At the end of the bouyed channel, as her tran-sit bearings came into line, she turned to starboard, heading out past the old sea forts built on their spits of rock against a possible French invasion in the middle years of the century, heading through Spithead to make on an easterly course towards

St Catherine's Point, then south around the Isle of Wight into the English Channel. The weather was still fair, with no more than a fresh wind blowing as the hands were fallen out from their stations and the sea watches set.

Two days later, with the Channel and the Lizard behind them, they passed Ushant into the Bay of Biscay. With the glass falling now, but with current weather conditions still favourable, Captain Fitzsimmons ordered his first gunnery practice, to bring his guns' crews to a high pitch of efficiency before arrival in the Gulf of Guinea.

Chapter 3

"GOOD morning, Mr Richards."

"Good morning, sir."

Captain Fitzsimmons sniffed the breeze, scanned the sky. "The Bay is not behaving normally, I think. Good weather before Ushant and good weather after as well is unusual, and we're lucky."

"The glass, sir—" This was Halfhyde, Officer of the Watch.

"Is Falling, Mr Halfhyde, as I am well aware, but Daily Orders as published will be adhered to nevertheless."

"Very good, sir."

Fitzsimmons frowned. "Mr Halfhyde?"

"Sir?"

"I think you have been ashore too long. Kindly do not tell me my orders are very good. Had I any doubt on the point, I would not have given them."

"I'm sorry, sir."

Looming over Halfhyde, pulling at his own beard, Captain Fitzsimmons glanced again at the sky and sea. The surface was flat and oily, but there was the long swell usually produced by the Bay of Biscay. This, in the Captain's view, would add spice to the gun drill, making it into more of an evolution than would have been the case on a level, motionless deck. He said, "Mr

Halfhyde, if you please, pipe the guns' crews to muster and ammunition parties to close up."

Halfhyde saluted. "Aye, aye, sir. Carry on, bosun's mate."

The bosun's mate saluted and went down the ladder from the bridge at the rush. Soon the pipes began shrilling throughout the ship, sending men hurrying to their stations at the guns and at the ammunition hoists from the magazines deep below the waterline. Below the open navigating bridge, the two six-inch guns on the gun deck abaft the fo'c'sle came alive. Under the orders of the captains of the guns, the painted canvas weather-protective covers were removed and the tompions taken out of the muzzles. There was much shouting from the gun captains and the gunner's mates as the crews gave the machinery a preliminary run through, the gunlayers busily turning hand-wheels to raise and depress, and give right and left deflection, to the great grey barrels. Mr Fasting, the gunner, and Mr Hawke, gunnery lieutenant, were everywhere at once: all bustle and loud mouth, St Vincent Halfhyde thought sardonically, looking down from the comparative peace of the bridge. St Vincent Halfhyde, willing enough to admit the truth of the gunnery enthusiasts' frequently and eloquently made point that the whole reason for a ship's existence was to be a floating platform for the guns, nevertheless held fast to the counter-point that it was the plain seamen, the salt horses, who in fact took the guns to the firing position and then, if they had chosen to qualify as seamen gunners, did the actual firing of them too. In his professional life Halfhyde had two passions, and two only, navigation and seamanship, an interest in naval history running these two a close third. The story of the British Navy, ever one of heroism and sacrifice, undoubtedly included many immortal deeds of bravery performed by gunners, but many more, in Halfhyde's reading at all events, performed less obtrusively by the simple seaman in his endless daily work of keeping the seas in all the varieties of weather that God could send to torment him. His predecessor, the unfortunate Lewis, had been but one example. Being swept overboard was usually a fairly final act. So was falling from aloft in the days of the old sailing navy, to land in a mess of blood, split flesh, and smashed bone on the unyielding deck or across a gunwhale.

Below him now, two midshipmen were in view, one to each of the forward guns, "A" and "B" guns. On "B" gun was the small wart who had joined with him, Mr Runcorn, looking thrilled to the marrow and mightily important, and trying not to show that he was about to hear the terrible noise of a six-inch gun for the very first time. St Vincent Halfhyde came away from the standard compass where he had been keeping a prudent eye on the Aurora's course, and leaned over the fore guard-rail. A word now would not be construed as undue favouritism.

"Good morning, Mr Runcorn," he called in a strong voice.

"Oh! Good morning, sir!" A smart salute accompanied the words as the wart looked up Godwards.

"Remember Trafalgar, Mr Runcorn."

"Yes, sir, thank you, sir."

An impish smile crossed Halfhyde's long face and he called down again. "Mr Runcorn, the lack of time to himself accorded a wart must never stop him trying to attain the acme of personal cleanliness."

"Sir?" The wart was puzzled.

"Mr Runcorn, I think you have not shaved your face this morning."

"Oh! I'm sorry, sir!" A hand felt smooth cheeks, and Halfhyde grinned dismissingly. His point had been made and the result was clear to see. Mr Runcorn, now a man in the eyes of his god, began to strut and to chivvy the gun's crew as any other man set in authority would. The day would now go better for one wart at least.

Though this was to be a full scale shoot with live charges and projectiles, there was of course no target. From the navigating bridge the fall of shot would be noted, and bearings taken to give some indication, however rudimentary, of the gunlayers' prowess when ordered to lay on a particular compass point. The main object of the exercise, as Captain Fitzsimmons had made clear, was to accustom the gunners to actual firing conditions and to increase the speed with which the guns would be fired and reloaded and fired again.

When the first executive order was given, Halfhyde crammed his fingers in his ears and earned a disparaging look from Fitzsimmons—who could, if he so wished, Halfhyde thought, suffer burst eardrums and deafness. It was up to no one but himself. Even through the fingers, the racket was appalling. Looking down at Mr Runcorn, Halfhyde saw that the wart had been badly shaken and looked as though he didn't know if he were coming or going, as his gun's crew, shouting still like all gunners, for no apparent reason, bustled about the machinery behind shield, throwing-off the muzzle to a point 33 degrees from the ship's centre line and then lowering it down to the loading tubes that slanted up from the main deck.

Behind Halfhyde on the bridge, Fitzsimmons was having sharp words with Mr Hawke. The great plumes of water that had risen from the Bay of Biscay had been in themselves satisfactory evidence that the guns had delivered their shells, but they were all in the wrong places. St Vincent Halfhyde's reading of the newspapers, whilst unemployed in London, had led him to the belief that the gunnery of the German Emperor's navy was much superior to that of Queen Victoria's, and here, it seemed, was the proof. This, however, was not a tactful moment in which to bring the press to the attention of either Fitzsimmons or Hawke. In any case, the Russians, not the Germans, were to be their possible adversaries when they reached the Bight of Benin . . .

"Mr Hawke, you must do better than this," the Captain was saying. "In the meantime, make sure that you have a check on the timing for reloading."

"Aye, aye, sir."

"There lies the crux of efficient firing, Mr Hawke. A slow ship has not the *time* to hit anything—even if the aim should be good! Bear that in mind, if you please, constantly."

"I shall, sir, you may be sure of it." Hawke left the bridge, and could be heard thereafter in deep conversation with Mr Fasting, the gunner. Ginger was to be put into the reloading operation. Mr Fasting and his mates began more than a degree of hazing, Mr Fasting himself, though merely a warrant officer, not forbearing to use harsh words to the warts as well as the men. Mr Runcorn, Halfhyde noticed, began to shake; and then finally, as the day wore on and the constant shattering explosions of the charges battered at his ears, he became a jelly that could do no more than gape and dither and be pushed out of the way by the energetic movements of the captain of the gun, an indignity that did not escape the eye of Captain Fitzsimmons. During one of the vital reloading operations, by which time—for it was now afternoon—the light was beginning to fade and the weather to show signs of deteriorating to the south, Fitzsimmons ordered Mr Runcorn to report in person to the bridge.

"It is not good enough, Mr Runcorn. You are there to take charge, not to be thrust aside by the captain of the gun, a mere rating. You will *take* charge, Mr Runcorn, is that understood?"

"Yes, sir." Mr Runcorn, white in the face, quaked. Had he not entered the Navy, he would at this moment be some prefect's fag, toasting crumpets in a comfortable study behind old stone walls, as safe as those walls themselves. Even the headmaster of Eton paled into total insignificance when compared with the captain of a ship at sea.

"Very well, you may carry on, and if there is further indecision your name will be entered in the log."

"Yes, sir." Mr Runcorn saluted and turned away, but was called back, thus preserving his life.

Fitzsimmons said, "The captain of the gun is to be placed in the Commander's report, Mr Runcorn, charged with insubordinate and contemptuous behaviour towards yourself."

"Oh, but sir—" This was sheer bravery, and was at once stepped upon.

"Mr Runcorn," thunderous tones said, "do you dare to argue with me?"

The response was perforce prompt. "Oh, no, sir!"

Fitzsimmons had opened his mouth to speed the wart back to his gun, when there was a tremendous explosion from just before the bridge, upon which all personnel were blown flat by the shock-wave, a blast of heat, and blinding smoke in which red flame licked greedily. Shaken, deafened, St Vincent Halfhyde staggered to his feet. He was, in fact, so deafened that he failed to hear his own voice, shouting out for the fire parties to come forward at the rush. A moment later the bosun's calls began, piping the fire parties to the fore part of the ship and to the loading tubes below on the main deck.

The dead, which included Mr Hawke who was fragmented almost beyond recognition and who had needed a bloody scooping into a sheet of canvas, were removed by the stretcher parties. The Fleet Surgeon attended the wounded, brought with all speed to the sick bay. An investigation was at once put in hand. This investigation, its result duly logged, revealed that "B" gun had blown up on reloading. When the fresh charge and projectile had been rammed up the bore under hydraulic power, the loading crews on the main deck had—as was customary with the old muzzle-loaders—known nothing of what was taking place on the deck above their heads. Up top, behind the gun shield, the crew's reactions had been virtually pulped by the constant explosions of the prolonged exercise and they were reacting in the fashion of mindless automatons, more or less as was in fact expected of them, and tragedy had ensued. At "B" gun, after reloading, the pulling of the firing lanyard had failed to ignite the detonator in the tube, with the result that the gun had misfired, a fact that in the general confusion brought about by long sustained firing, and the close proximity of the exploding charges from "A" gun, had gone utterly and criminally unnoticed by "B" gun's crew. Thus, the charge and the shell were still in the gun-barrel when it was depressed for its next reloading, and when the gun was again fired the breech had burst under the impact of the double loading. Besides killing the gun's crew, and injuring the adjacent men on "A" gun, the blast, travelling down the hatchway behind the gun, had caused havoc on the main deck, badly injuring some twenty men.

Fitzsimmons, pale but hard of face, received that evening the enquiry findings from the Commander. "This will be reported to the Admiralty from Gibraltar," he said. "It will make fine reading for the Ordnance Department at Woolwich!"

"Let us trust they act on it, sir," Gordon said with much feeling, "and take out all our muzzle-loaders for replacement by breech-loaders! This could never happen with breech-loaders."

"True, but there had been carelessness nevertheless."

"Unpunishable carelessness, sir."

"What?"

The Commander said soberly, "Sir, the men are all dead."

"Except for Mr Midshipman Runcorn, Commander. I am not, I hope, a vindictive man—this will not be overplayed. The midshipman is young, and this is his first ship. But he cannot escape all the consequences of not having had his wits about him, Commander."

"I agree, sir. But we should remember he was on the bridge when the burst occurred."

Fitzsimmons nodded. "Of course. But he was the midshipman on the gun, and by his earlier conduct failed to contribute to the crew's efficiency." He glanced up at his bulkhead clock. "Pipe the hands to supper, if you please, Commander. I take it they can be spared now?"

"The ship's cleaned up, sir. All blood removed, all repairable damage made good. Yes, they can go to supper." The Commander hesitated. "Sir, does this affect our orders in any way?"

Fitzsimmons looked astonished. "Great heavens, Commander, by no means! We shall put into Gibraltar for coal as normal, and to land such of the wounded as the Fleet Surgeon can't cope with. With luck, we shall get replacements for the dead. Whether or not we get them, Commander—and in spite of the loss of a gun—we proceed in execution of our orders for the Bight of Benin."

"Aye, aye, sir." The Commander rubbed at tired eyes. It had been a day of strain, and the hour was now late. "Do you expect any news of the Russian squadron?"

"In Gibraltar? Who knows—I don't! I know only this: we must get Halfhyde there as ordered, and as soon as possible, lest the situation worsens."

"And the ship's company, sir? Will you clear lower deck and tell them the facts behind our orders?"

Fitzsimmons pulled at his beard and answered coldly, "My dear sir, it has never been my custom to acquaint the lower deck with what I am told privily at the Admiralty."

That night the weather changed utterly. By six bells in the first watch the Commander had battened down and ordered the life-lines rigged fore and aft. Men on the upper deck, battered by a strong wind and flung seas, moved with difficulty about their various tasks, taking good care not to follow the late Lieutenant Lewis into a watery grave. Below decks the atmosphere was cold and thick, wet from the clothing of men coming down from above. Such was the strength of the wind and the heavy beam-sea roll, coupled with the basic swell of the Bay of

Biscay, that the galley fires had been drawn as a precaution: no hot drinks, no cocoa for the watchkeepers on the upper deck or in the engine- and boiler-rooms. The hope was that if the conditions persisted, the Captain would authorize an extra rum issue next forenoon to keep the ice cold winter seas from the men's bones. Down below, the Fleet Engineer, Mr Evans, was himself on the starting-platform, watching, with his Senior Engineer, the various dials and pressure-gauges, watching steamy valves, watching the indicator from the navigating bridge, the clock hand that would transmit to the vibrating, noise-dominated engine-room the instant orders of the Officer of the Watch. Around the heaving engines, keeping their feet with difficulty on the greasy deck plating, men moved about with oil-cans, looking, feeling for over-heating, probing the long noses of the cans here and there, keeping all bearings running efficiently. In the boiler-rooms, the half-naked stokers poured sweat as they shovelled their coal, banging down the bunker-chutes in chunky showers, into the redly gaping mouths of the furnaces. In the sick bay the assistant surgeon kept a constant vigil, shaking his head at the cries of badly burned men, busying himself and his sick-berth attendants with soothing ointments, doing what little he could to ease great pain.

In his hammock Mr Runcorn lay sleepless, listening to the same ship noises as was Lieutenant St Vincent Halfhyde in his bunk nearby. In the gunroom that night the wart had suffered much. Mr Dalrymple-Martin, sub of the gunroom, having heard a thing or two, had dropped hints that the wretched little wart, having let his gun's crew and the ship down by ignominious funk of gunfire, would have much to answer for when the Captain found the time. Mr Runcorn, admitting in the privacy of his hammock a degree of undeniable fear that had left him without the wit to do more than stand in the way and stare, wept. He couldn't help it. Three days after joining his first ship as a midshipman, and he had already failed to act the man he was, despite his lack of years, supposed to be. He was degraded, an ignoble thing who may have been responsible for many deaths and injuries, a thing any Captain would loathe on sight from now to eternity. He felt almost suicidal; his career lay in ruins. Following upon the urge to suicide came a new feeling. He hated the sea and didn't care any more. He would follow the perennial advice to sailors: he would buy a farm, walking inland with an oar over his shoulder until the first man asked him what it was he was carrying. There he would stay, far from ships, water, captains and sub-lieutenants, and deep feelings of inadequacy.

Wartlike, he managed to survive the night and at four in the morning proceeded to the bridge to take over once again as Midshipman of the Watch. He found Mr Halfhyde there, taking over the watch from another of the Lieutenants. As soon as he could do so, Mr Halfhyde talked to him. Mr Halfhyde didn't make the mistake of sympathizing, but yet managed to ease his hurts and restore some of his self-respect. The wart was grateful. The ending of the watch, however, was still hell, for it meant breakfast in the gunroom, and more of Mr Dalrymple-Martin's tongue.

But his real ordeal came at four bells in the forenoon watch, when, the weather having moderated a little so that at least the decks were dry, he was sent for by the Captain to report on the quarterdeck. Here, in loud tones that carried to groups of seamen working on the upper deck, Fitzsimmons dressed him down.

"Damnable, disgraceful . . . reactions of a babe in arms . . . not fit to sweep out the heads . . . failure to take charge is the very worst sin, bar active treason or disobedience, any officer can commit. Men have died . . . words fail me, Mr Runcorn! However, in view of your lack of experience I shall be lenient, and pray to God I'm later proved right to have been so. You will go at once to the fore topmast, Mr Runcorn, and remain upon the crosstrees until I order you down. I repeat the words *at once*. This means that you will have no time in which to provide yourself with an oilskin."

Head low, Mr Runcorn sped forward to climb the foremast. Halfhyde, coming aft along the alleyway, saw him and enquired his errand; and saw also the Sub-Lieutenant concealed inside the after screen, where the open door had given him the opportunity of overhearing the Captain's remarks.

Halfhyde stopped. "A word in your ear, Mr Dalrymple-Martin."

"Sir?" The Sub-Lieutenant came forward and halted.

"Mr Runcorn has had, or rather is about to undergo, his punishment—for what, I fail to comprehend—however, that is by the way. What I have to say is this, Mr Dalrymple-Martin: I shall never in any way interfere with your authority in the gun-room, which is your concern alone. At the same time, I must impress upon you that one punishment is quite enough. Do you understand me?"

The sub's small eyes stared back, red and angry, a mean and insubordinate look. "I believe I do, sir. You are ordering me not to haze that wart."

Halfhyde laughed. "Oh, no! Come, Mr Dalrymple-Martin, there is no *order* about this, it is simply advice. But it is good advice, Mr Dalrymple-Martin, and should be commended to you most strongly. Discipline is one thing, bullying is another—and is one that rouses the worst in me, I confess. And if I were you, Mr Dalrymple-Martin, I would remove that aggrieved and mutinous look from my face—and quickly!" His colour high, Halfhyde went on his way, passing through the door to the quarterdeck.

Chapter 4

FROM the foretop, Mr Runcorn, shivering like a castanet in a keen wind, clutching the thin topmast for his life against the twenty-degree roll resulting from the swell, looked down at six bells in the forenoon watch at one of the Royal Navy's grimmest ceremonies afloat: the committal of the dead to the deep. This took place from the starboard side of the quarterdeck, the lee side away from the bite of the offshore wind. The Captain and all off-watch executive officers were present, with the seamen divisions fallen in behind and along the after part of the midship superstructure—no engineers to bring whiffs of oil and coaldust to the clean day. This was upper-deck business, and Fitzsimmons had made the fact plain to the Fleet Engineer. The six corpses, sewn into their canvas jackets with the last stitch, in accordance with seafaring custom, run through the dead man's nose, lay in two rows facing the ship's side, beneath the folds of the White Ensign. Facing them from a scrubbed wooden grating acting as a dais, stood the cruiser's chaplain in cassock and surplice. Simply and strongly, the chaplain read the service while the ship's company stood with bared, bowed heads. The cruiser, lying with her main engines respectfully stopped, rolled and heaved as the deep-sea swell passed beneath her keel. As the padre came to the actual committal service, four men lifted the first of the corpses, that of a young able-seaman, laid it, held still, on a plank slightly tilted towards the sea from a section of the deck where the guard-rail had been temporarily removed. The padre's voice went on, loud but sad.

"We therefore commit his body to the deep, to be turned into corruption, looking for the resurrection of the body, when the Sea shall give up her dead . . ."

At a signal from the chief bosun's mate, standing by the plank, the bearers gave the wood a sharp tilt. The corpse shot from under the White Ensign, which was held fast at the inboard end, and, bending a little in the middle, plummeted down into the Bay of Biscay. For a few seconds it could be seen, a dirty white in the water, then the seas closed over it and it was gone. The others followed, the last of all being the late gunnery lieutenant, Mr Hawke. Halfhyde, watching from his place behind the Captain, gave a small smile, twisted, sardonic. Naval routine held: in life, the least important went into a boat first so as not to keep his seniors waiting, but on disembarking it was the other way round—seniors first. Hawke, closely followed by the gunner's mate, was all set to beard St Peter first. The last committal made, there was a brief silence, then the men's voices rose, singing the sailors' hymn, "For Those in Peril on the Sea." As always, it was moving. Halfhyde sang strongly and with sincerity. When the service ended, the Commander caught Fitzsimmons's eye. The Captain nodded, and turned away, tall and angular, hands clasped behind his back. The Commander in his turn nodded at the First Lieutenant, one MacMahon who called the ship's company to attention.

"Ship's company will dismiss. Ship's company, turn for'ard, dismiss!" There was a movement of flapping bell-bottoms, then the rushing patter of bare feet going forward at the double. The First Lieutenant turned to the Master-at-Arms, chief of the ship's police. "All right, Master, you may pipe Up Spirits."

"Aye, aye, sir."

The bosun's calls sounded for the breaking out of the rum casks for the day's standard issue. Halfhyde, going below to his cabin where he had certain work to do, smiled again with a touch of bitterness. "Up Spirits," he thought, "but stand fast the Holy Ghost . . ."

On his lonely, isolated platform, in his public disgrace, Mr Runcorn shivered uncontrollably.

In his cabin, Halfhyde, with only a part of his mind on the Russian text-book he was ploughing through, considered once again the orders he had been given at the Admiralty. They were in part precise, in part vague. He was not, the Rear-Admiral had said—and this had been an order to Fitzsimmons rather than to Halfhyde—to be involved unnecessarily in the ship's routine. He was to keep his watch and be attentive to such duties as might befall him as a seaman when necessary for the ship's safety; but he was to undertake no other duties such as would normally be given other executive officers—responsibility for the wellbeing of the men of a particular division, for example, general ship cleanliness, care of boats or guns or navigational equipment and so on. His appointment not being normal, he was to be free for his particular duties, which would begin as soon as the *Aurora* arrived off the Bight of Benin on the West African coast, where lay the Russian cruiser *Grand Duke Alexis*. The Rear-Admiral, in reference to a bitter period in Halfhyde's past, had gone on, "At the time you were in Russian hands, Mr Halfhyde, there was danger of war between Britain and Russia, as you know."

"Yes, sir."

"For some years now that danger has appeared to recede, which is pleasing both to Her Majesty and to Lord Salisbury. Now there are matters that suggest the clock is being turned back, Mr Halfhyde. With your particular experience, we believe you can assist a very great deal."

"We, sir? May I ask, who is *we?*"

The Rear-Admiral, after a quick look at Fitzsimmons, said quietly, "Lord Salisbury, Mr Halfhyde."

"The Prime Minister himself?"

"And Her Majesty too."

Halfhyde had given a gasp. "The Queen has been consulted on *my* appointment?"

"Yes, that is the case," the Rear-Admiral had continued, saying something about Her Majesty and her personal relationship with the Russian court. Halfhyde, blood drumming in his ears, had scarcely listened as he should have done. It was no wonder Fitzsimmons was looking so damn stony! His new lieutenant was to be only nominally. That lieutenant's appointment was out of his hands—therefore so was his dismissal. It was an intriguing situation for any lieutenant to find himself in. There were dangers, embarrassments, but also potential honours in it. It was indeed seldom that the movements of a mere lieutenant of the British Fleet became of personal moment to the Queen herself!

Halfhyde, in his small and stuffy cabin aboard the *Aurora,* thinking of all the Rear-Admiral had said, closed the Russian textbook with a snap and rose to his feet. He leaned across the bunk to stare out through his port at the lifting swell, the lifting and falling swell that at times hoisted the cruiser to its peak so that the men aboard her seemed to look down a long, long valley of water spreading into the far distance, and then next moment plunged the vessel into the depths so that it lay at the bottom of a mountainside, in a curious quiet eeriness, with the force of the wind cut off by the great wall of water. Halfhyde was no stranger to this, any more than he was to the Russians. Counting his cadet's time, he had been at sea since the age of thirteen but for two periods in his life: the time passed on half-pay, and the year in Russian hands. He had been a midshipman in the old sloop *Cloud,* last of the sail-rigged steamers, when, some years after the European congress in Berlin where peace had been secured by Disraeli and Salisbury, an impetuous captain who happened to have drunk too much whisky had ordered his guns to fire upon a Russian warship entering the Bosphorus from the Sea of Marmora. The Russian had opened on the *Cloud,* which had blown up, leaving only three survivors, among them Mr Midshipman Halfhyde. They had all been picked up by the Russians. The other two had died soon after from their injuries and Halfhyde had been taken through the Bosphorus to the naval part of Sevastopol, where one Prince Gorsinski, a relative of the Czar of all the Russias, had been the admiral in charge of the dockyard. Halfhyde, brought before the admiral in person, had impressed the Russian by his self-possession and dignified bearing. Prince Gorsinski had seemed to bear the British midshipman no malice. Halfhyde, without any ceremony, had been bundled off to Siberia by order from the court at St Petersburg, but after only two months in the bitter Arctic cold had been extricated by Prince Gorsinski and brought back to Sevastopol, where, refusing to give his parole, he had been confined to more civilized quarters, even, as an embryo officer, being assigned a servant to wait upon him. He had had many long conversations with Gorsinski, growing to know and like the Russian aristocrat, even though he saw with his own eyes the savage treatment accorded to other prisoners when from time to time Turkish ships of war were captured. During this enforced period in Russian naval hands, Halfhyde learned a good deal about his host country and her ships, and he learned to speak and read Russian. A little more than a year after his capture, he managed to escape, made his way into Turkey and thence home to England, where a grateful country took no particular notice of his return, other than to have him questioned somewhat perfunctorily at the Admiralty and then to appoint him to HMS *Arrow* on the West African coast to complete his time as a midshipman. Now, it seemed, the knowledge and experience he had gained in Russia were to be utilized.

The facts behind his mission were simple enough, and had been plainly put at the Admiralty: "We believe the Russians to have put landing-parties ashore in the Fishtown area of the Bight of Benin, and to have constructed fortifications. Also— and this is why we lack information, so cannot be precise as to our beliefs—they have allowed only their own nationals any contact with the shore. Vessels of other flags have been instructed to confine their crews aboard."

"There is no contact with the shore in any case, sir, except by means of the native-manned canoes."

"Yes, yes, I, too, am aware of the problems created by the surf, Mr Halfhyde, thank you. The fact appears to be that the

Russians have prevented any contact by the natives with ships in the anchorage, while, as you know, ships of any size cannot cross the bar in safety." The Rear-Admiral seemed to go off at a tangent. "An inhospitable country—desolate and full of savages, men who indulge in human sacrifice!"

"Indeed, sir. In which case," Halfhyde had asked with his tongue in his cheek, "why do we not leave them to sacrifice the Russians?"

It had been the wrong thing to say. Anger flashed from the Rear-Admiral's eye. "We have our trading-posts on the Gold Coast, in Sierra Leone, the Gambia, and the Oil Rivers Protectorate to consider. Any Russian force based upon the Bight of Benin could have the most disastrous effect, and I dare say the general apparent unsuitability of the place—the foul weather, the difficulties of landing men and supplies—this may have commended itself to the Russians in so far as it would appear to us unlikely that they would use such an appalling area. Nevertheless, we believe that they have done so. And apart from our responsibilities to our trading-posts, Mr Halfhyde, we have a need to preserve intact our sea route to the Cape. So you will do me the courtesy of not attempting to make jokes, sir!"

"Aye, aye, sir," Halfhyde had answered submissively but with a spark of laughter in his eye. The Rear-Admiral was pompous and could do with a prick. The intended British counter-action had then been outlined. The *Aurora* was to be despatched to watch proceedings, to land Halfhyde, and to prevent the Russian cruiser from sailing out of the Bight, the latter operation being put into effect only if Halfhyde should fail in his primary mission.

"Which is?" Halfhyde enquired.

The reply had been evasive. "You will be informed in detail by Captain Fitzsimmons after your ship sails from Portsmouth, Mr Halfhyde. It is enough for me to say now that your experience as a pilot in the waters of the Bight may be put to good use, and that your knowledge of the Russian language, and indeed of the Russian Navy, will also be of value."

Vague orders indeed! Still looking out from the tight-shut port, Halfhyde's reflections were bitter. So far there had been no word from Captain Fitzsimmons. For Halfhyde's part, he believed strongly that dirty work was in the offing and that the Board of Admiralty, needing clean hands, had no wish to be too closely associated with it, just in case the plan, whatever it was to be, should fail. It was ever thus. The whole Board would claim their part with alacrity if the result should be a success.

Fitzsimmons came on to the navigating bridge at six bells in the afternoon watch.

"Tell me," he said to the Officer of the Watch, "how long has Mr Runcorn been aloft?"

"Four hours, sir."

Fitzsimmons nodded briefly. "Then he may come down." He raised his voice, staring aloft towards the foretop. "Mr Runcorn!" He paused, then called again. He frowned. "The boy doesn't answer."

"The weather's cold, sir." The Officer of the Watch, huddled into oilskins, looked blue.

"I am aware of the temperature, Mr Cotterrell." Fitzsimmons called again. Behind him, bare feet pattered up the ladder from the midship superstructure. A small, elderly man, a quid of tobacco fairly obvious in his cheek, a length of spun yarn looped round one big toe, came round to the Captain's front and saluted.

"Beg pardon, sir."

"What is it, Brinthwaite?"

Leading-seaman Brinthwaite, coxswain of the Captain's galley, transferred his tobacco across his tongue before speaking again. "Permission to go aloft, sir."

"Aloft, Brinthwaite? What for, man, what for?"

"Young gennelman's likely frozen to t'top, sir."

"Nonsense!" Fitzsimmons bristled, square beard out-thrust, but Brinthwaite stood his ground firmly.

"Beg pardon, sir, but 'e's as a nasty white look and 'e don't move a perishin' eyebrow beggin' yer pardon, sir. If I go up t'mast, sir, I can bring t'young gennelman down to t'deck, sir."

Fitzsimmons glared, looked aloft again, then changed his mind. "Aloft with you, then!" he snapped. He turned on his heel and left the bridge. Brinthwaite, chewing hard on his quid, slid down the ladder behind him and ran for the ratlines. He went up like a monkey, fast and sure, and the men below saw him reach the foretop, swinging outwards from the futtock-shrouds as the cruiser rolled hard to port, nimble and confident. They saw him take the wart in his arms, and speak to him, and then massage warmth into half-frozen arms and legs. Brinthwaite, muttering to himself in a harsh voice about callous bastards who forgot they'd once been first-voyage midshipman their effing selves, tended the teeth-chattering wart for the best part of fifteen minutes before starting to ease him down the lubber's-hole after himself. Whilst doing this he had a surprise.

The little wart resisted the lubber's-hole, not wishing to incur further spite from Mr Dalrymple-Martin. "Thank you very much, Brinthwaite," he said. "I'll use the futtock-shrouds."

"Take care, Mr Runcorn, sir."

"I'm all right," the wart said squeakily. Down he came, feet groping for the ratlines just above Brinthwaite's descending head. From the guard-rail abreast the bridge he jumped down to the deck. "Thank you," he said, meeting the leading-seaman's eye. "I could have managed, you know."

"Yessir," Brinthwaite said promptly, accompanying the words with a grin and a wink. "It was just that you 'ad cloth ears, an' didn't 'ear t'Captain, sir." He reached out a fatherly hand. "You'll do, young sir. No lubber'd 'ave come down t'futtock-shrouds, wi' 'is arse 'anging free over t'Bay o' bloody Biscay, sir. Just you remember what Brinthwaite says, sir."

The wart nodded gratefully, reported to the navigating bridge, and scuttled below.

Three days later, with her ports now open and a clean fresh wind blowing through the mess decks and flats, the *Aurora,* past Cape Trafalgar with its memories of Admiral Lord Nelson, came round Tarifa Point to head across Gibraltar Bay for the dockyard. Fitzsimmons ordered his number to be made to the Rear-Admiral commanding the naval base. In reply a string of flags crept up the signal halliards of the shore station, to be read off by the yeoman of signals.

"From Rear-Admiral, sir," the yeoman sang out, closing his telescope with a final snap. "Proceed alongside coaling berth. Report personally as soon as you have secured."

"Acknowledge," Fitzsimmons said briefly. He caught

Halfhyde's eye, and at once looked away again. Both men knew well enough what the reason was for the Flag Officer's hurry. Fitzsimmons, conning his ship towards the coaling berth at the north-western corner of the dockyard, spoke again, this time to the Officer of the Watch. "Inform the First Lieutenant, if you please, Mr Richards. No leave is to be piped, at least until I've reported to the Flag."

With an hour of arrival in the lee of the huge brown mass that was the Rock of Gibraltar, first military outpost of the Empire, the ship was black coaldust from stem to stern, from truck to waterline. The very air was thick with it. Though the lower deck and the flats and cabin alleyways had been, so far as was ever possible, sealed off, and all ventilators shut, the filth penetrated, and when the sweating officers and men returned to their quarters they would find a film of gritty black over all. In the meantime, they worked. The business of replenishing the bunkers was always treated as an evolution. All personnel took part in one way or another. When ships of a fleet were in company, it was a matter of pride to complete coaling first, so the men worked like demons, black as Mephistopheles himself, sending the coal thundering down the chutes to clang and echo in the steel bunkers. The *Aurora,* with a total bunkering capacity of 400 tons, giving a range of 6000 miles steaming at 10 knots, was in fact far from empty; and the operation was complete, and the decks were already being washed down, when Captain Fitzsimmons returned from his duty call upon the Flag and came up the accommodation-ladder from his galley in cocked hat, sword and epaulettes. He had a preoccupied look. Returning the salutes of Officer of the Watch, corporal of the gangway, bosun's mates and side boys, he spoke peremptorily.

"The Commander and the Fleet Engineer, if you please, in my cabin immediately."

"Aye, aye, sir. *Boy!*"

A side boy went off at the double. Fitzsimmons said, "And no leave to be piped. The ship will be going to sea at four bells."

Ten minutes later, St Vincent Halfhyde was sent for to the cuddy.

Chapter 5

AS Halfhyde answered the summons from the Captain, the ship was already being prepared again for sea. The galley was hoisted to the davits and secured by the watch. Word had spread around the ship that no crew replacements were available at Gibraltar and, in view of their hasty departure, no new six-inch gun could be provided and fitted in time.

Halfhyde, entering the Captain's cabin, found Fitzsimmons at his roll-top desk.

"You sent for me, sir?"

"I have your orders now, Mr Halfhyde."

"Provided by Gibraltar, sir?"

"Provided by the Admiralty, Mr Halfhyde, but embellished by certain intelligence made known to me whilst ashore."

"I see. May I have the two in separate compartments, sir?"

"What?"

"The orders and the embellishments, sir."

Fitzsimmons's colour rose above the square beard. "Are you being impertinent, sir?"

"No, sir. Merely prudent in my own interest. Orders I must presumably obey. Embellishments have, to me, the ring of being . . . no more than advice."

"I do not like *clever* officers," Fitzsimmons said in an angry tone. Then he frowned, and began tapping on his desk, and

looking, Halfhyde thought, a shade uncertain and less trucu-
lent. "No more do I like intrigue. I am a simple sailor, Mr
Halfhyde—and all this smells to me of intrigue, and of business better left to diplomats. I prefer an open fight."

"And I too, sir." Halfhyde said promptly. "This was none of
my seeking."

Fitzsimmons looked keenly at Halfhyde, frowning again and
pulling at his beard. Then he said abruptly, "I know that's true
at least. Sit down, Mr Halfhyde."

"Thank you, sir." Halfhyde sat in a leather armchair set
across the cabin from the desk. Fitzsimmons swivelled to face
him, then spoke in a low voice, as if to himself. "I have a feeling the open fight must come, though we are under orders, you
and I, to prevent it to the best of our ability. In that, lies the
nub of your own orders, Halfhyde."

Halfhyde's eyebrows rose. At last, he thought, he's dropped
the mister in the privacy of his cabin! Halfhyde made no
response and Fitzsimmons went on, "Those orders, the orders
from the Admiralty, instruct you to land on the Slave Coast, in
the region of the Benin and Escravos rivers, and to make
your way to Fishtown as a deserter from the British Fleet. In
Fishtown, you are to make contact with the Russians. Your
orders are to find out all you can about the Russian intentions
and the likely deployment of any force, naval or military,
which they may anticipate using in the Bight; also to obtain the
fullest information in regard to the fortifications erected by the
Russians—their personnel, their armament, their defensive
strength, thickness of walls, and so on."

"Yes, sir. May I ask how I reach the coast?"

Fitzsimmons said, "You will be put over the side with a

baulk of timber when the ship is twenty miles off the mouth of the Benin river."

"On a baulk of timber, did you say, sir?"

"Yes, a baulk of timber."

"In the Atlantic rollers, sir—the surf of the Bight coast? By God, sir, this sounds to me like madness, the talk of a clerk rather then a seaman—"

"Risks," Fitzsimmons said, holding up a hand, "are part of an officer's life, and must be accepted. Do you fear such a passage through the surf?"

Halfhyde snapped, "I would be a fool if I didn't!"

"But you will do it?"

There was a pause, during which Halfhyde, in his mind's eye, saw the terrible lines of spray-capped, racing, surf roaring on to the African coast, but saw also a vision of Camden Town and Mrs Mavitty. "Oh, I'll do it," he said dourly. "What of the ship, sir, when I am going inshore on my baulk of timber?"

"I shall stand out to sea again immediately, to remain in station, but cruising, outside the Gulf of Guinea. There will be a daily rendezvous position, yet to be worked out between us. When you have the required information, you will rejoin in that rendezvous area."

Halfhyde asked sardonically, "On my baulk of timber, sir? Which will, of course, be fitted with a standard compass and a signal mast?"

Fitzsimmons gave a frigid smile. "The method of your rejoining will be up to you, Mr Halfhyde, but you will be provided with a boat's compass and it should not be beyond the wit of an officer of resource to equip himself with a suitable boat."

"A war canoe, sir?" Halfhyde asked with a curl of his lips.

Shrugging indifferently, Fitzsimmons answered, "As you wish. They are known to be perfectly seaworthy."

There was a pause, then Halfhyde said, "So those are the orders. Are they in writing, sir?"

"No, they are verbal."

"How very convenient." Halfhyde's voice was acid. "In certain circumstances, sir, a deserter from the British Fleet can most conveniently be left to his fate, can he not? May I ask, sir, from which ship I shall have deserted—since I would assume it must not be the *Aurora,* in case she is reported to the Russian captain as lurking on station outside the Gulf, and a stinking rat is smelt?" Fitzsimmons nodded. "Yes, you're right. You'll have deserted from the *Diadem,* on passage from the Cape to the Medway. This will be substantiated if necessary. The *Diadem* is in fact on such a passage, and her captain will receive the necessary orders on arrival at Gibraltar."

Halfhyde, his long face seeming more sallow than ever, asked, "And now, sir, the embellishments?"

Fitzsimmons said, "I am informed by the Rear-Admiral that two more Russian cruisers passed through the Gibraltar strait forty-eight hours ago, steaming fast. An inward bound sloop later reported them as having turned to the southward in latitude thirty-five degrees north, longitude ten degrees west. From that we may draw our own conclusions, Mr Halfhyde. The cruisers are the *Romanov* and the *St Petersburg,* the former wearing the admiral's flag." Fitzsimmons paused, looking narrowly at Halfhyde. "The admiral is believed to be Prince Gorsinski."

"Gorsinski!" Halfhyde rose from his chair, staring down at the Captain. "Gorsinski! Then I take it we have been wasting our time, sir, for certainly I can't go ahead with my orders now."

"On the contrary, Mr Halfhyde—"

"But it's impossible! Impossible, I tell you—"

"Kindly lower your voice, Mr Halfhyde."

"Sir, this is the sheerest lunacy! Prince Gorsinski will get to hear of my presence, he will send for me, he will recognize me—and the whole stupid plot will become as clear as day."

"No, no. The reports of your captivity have been studied. Prince Gorsinski was well disposed towards you."

"Yes, until I escaped from him. That will scarcely have pleased him, and, in any case, he will quite fail to see me in the role of a deserter! I shall not be able to fool him, sir. If this business continues, then you not only sign my death warrant, but you also expose the Board of Admiralty as a set of utter dunderheads—and yourself as well!"

"Silence, sir!" Fitzsimmons was now on his feet as well, beard jutting. "If there is more impertinence, I shall order you to be placed in arrest until the time comes to—"

"To jettison me, sir, for that is what you will do."

Fitzsimmons waved impotent fists. "You will not be jettisoned! Have you no regard for your duty, for a proper patriotism?"

Halfhyde smiled insolently his face hard. "Patriotism, what is patriotism? Dr Johnson expressed the view that patriotism was the last refuge of the scoundrel—"

"Silence, sir! Damn you, be silent!" Fitzsimmons fumed. He stormed up and down the cabin for a full minute, apparently regaining control of his outraged feelings. Then he stopped and faced Halfhyde, still angry but calmer. He said, "I think you misunderstand. Prince Gorsinski may well talk more openly to you, since he knows you well."

"And since, also, he will be taking me back to Russia, and a probable sentence of death!"

"No." Fitzsimmons shook his head. "Do me the courtesy of believing that I have given this matter much thought, along with the Flag Officer in Gibraltar, who concurs in my decision to continue. Consider, Mr Halfhyde! If one of the Russian ships has aboard a British officer held prisoner, does this not give the Fleet an unarguable right to go in and get him out, and to use its guns—a right that will not be questioned anywhere in the world, as would any attempt to interfere with supposedly peaceful trading aspirations held by the Russians?" The Captain looked at Halfhyde coldly. "This links with another aspect—a serious one, I think you will agree."

"Well, sir?"

Fitzsimmons said, "Rumours have reached Gibraltar that certain traders, among them British nationals, have disappeared from Fishtown recently. They're believed to be held aboard the *Grand Duke Alexis*. Do you understand the import of that, Mr Halfhyde?"

Halfhyde nodded. "Yes, I think I do, sir. But what am I to do about it? Get them out single-handed?"

"No. In furtherance of the original orders from the Admiralty, you'll observe and confirm. When you rejoin in the rendezvous position, if you confirm that these traders are held prisoner, or in any sense at all against their will, then a course of action will be decided upon."

"And me? Are the Russians going to allow me out of Fishtown, with such certain knowledge in my head?"

"I refer to what I said earlier, Mr Halfhyde—you are a British officer. You may depend upon it, you'll not be left in Russian hands."

Halfhyde stared back. "I don't like this, sir. The Admiralty has not concurred, even if the admiral in Gibraltar has. Suppose I refuse—what then?"

Fitzsimmons shrugged. "It will be back to half-pay, my dear sir—or dismissal from Her Majesty's service."

The thick figure and the comfortable breasts of Mrs Mavitty obscured once again the gold-encrusted dignity of Captain Fitzsimmons.

Halfhyde, wrapped in a thick reefer jacket—for although they were coming into warmer seas now, the nights were cold still—was standing motionless in a corner of the navigating bridge, keeping that night's middle watch. His mind rioted. Fitzsimmons had been immovable, and the orders stood. In vain, Halfhyde had tried to make the point that the Admiralty's wishes would be grossly flouted if any cutting-out operation to retrieve him should lead to an exchange of gunfire. What could be more of a war situation than that? But Fitzsimmons had merely returned to his point that any capture of a British officer was a cast iron excuse. Halfhyde, admitting the point, was still unhappy. The whole affair was unsatisfactory and nasty, dangerous to himself in a most unsavoury way. As a deserter, he could in fact be left to his fate without any public outcry if the Admiralty should find it politically desirable to dissociate themselves, or if Captain Fitzsimmons, having second thoughts when the deed was done and he began to give weight to the expressed desires for peace of the Queen and Lord Salisbury, should after all deem it expedient to withdraw his fingers from the fire. Halfhyde knew that he would be putting his life and his reputation in the not over-friendly hands of Fitzsimmons, which was a risk in itself. A more probable risk, for Halfhyde had an innate belief in the basic decency of British seamen, was Prince Gorsinski. The Russian was no fool. In Halfhyde's view, no success could possibly attend his mission. The Admiralty, he was convinced, would have issued cancellation orders. As to the Flag Officer in Gibraltar, one Sir Thomas Layton, Halfhyde knew of him by repute: an old fossil, genial enough, but virtually senile, inclined to agree with anybody. Fitzsimmons would have had him eating out of his hand.

Why?

Was Fitzsimmons, in fact, deliberately jettisoning him? If so, where was his motive? Did it emanate from higher up? Halfhyde had made enemies and knew it. Though he found it difficult to see any of them behaving in such a way, he had a mind, now, to disobey, to reject that damned baulk of timber already being prepared by the carpenter's mates! He stared bleakly out from the bridge as the *Aurora* moved towards the South Atlantic to head down past Casablanca and the Canaries. He weighed the alternatives. Half-pay was half a life, a life of suspension in the midst of other men's bustle, a life of no progress and no promotion. Back to Mrs Mavitty, back to public bars and the dregs of London's stage doors, of lonely walks along city streets, far from the seabirds' cries and the starlit night skies, and the surge and roll of a ship? Back to clothes worn threadbare, to shoes that leaked, to excuses made to friends for not accepting unreturnable hospitality, to a life of well-meant lies told to maintain one's self respect? St Vincent Halfhyde, when on half-pay, had not accepted help from the farm in Wensleydale, nor had he wished to billet himself on his parents, thus confessing failure to maintain his position adequately. That was not Halfhyde's way. He had suffered, but he had suffered in silent isolation, an isolation as deep as that in which the *Aurora* was currently wrapped beneath the low-slung stars, though the sea had an isolation as different from that of half-pay as chalk from cheese . . .

The isolation was interrupted by footsteps and a voice. "Officer of the Watch, sir. Seven bells."

Halfhyde stirred. "Thank you, bosun's mate. Call the morning watch in ten minutes' time, if you please."

"Aye, aye, sir."

Soon the pipe sounded along the mess decks. Halfhyde visualized the busy bosun's mates below, passing along the slung hammocks with their cries of "Show a leg, show a leg there, rouse out, quickly now!" He checked the course and revolutions, and handed over a little before eight bells to his relief, Lieutenant Cotterrell. Going down the ladder, he met a wart hastening forward along the deck to relieve his opposite number.

"Good morning, Mr Runcorn."

"Oh—good morning, sir!"

"Enjoying life, Mr Runcorn?"

"Oh yes, sir!" Happiness a trifle forced? Halfhyde smiled in the darkness, full of fellow-feeling.

"Not thinking of deserting, by any chance, Mr Runcorn?"

"Sir?" The wart was puzzled, as well he might be, and Halfhyde laughed dismissingly, and went on his way aft along the silent deck, the dry deck, now free of those flinging tons of water, thinking his own thoughts. These had suddenly taken a very fresh and intriguing turn, and were to keep him sleepless in his bunk, tossing and turning, wondering, debating with himself, trying to see it from every angle, rigorously searching his mind to discover whether or not this new concept was no more than pure self-interest.

"A broadening experience," Halfhyde said to Fitzsimmons after Divisions, with the ship steaming south under all possible steam through a flat blue sea. The ship's company were now in white uniforms, with white covers over the blue caps of the officers.

"And a dangerous one, Mr Halfhyde."

"True, sir. But we're not deterred by thoughts of danger, are we?" Brightly, mockingly, Halfhyde smiled. "I am certain, sir, that it would give the mission, the objective, more chance of success. Much more. It's a better story, sir. Prince Gorsinski would be better convinced."

"Go over it again," Fitzsimmons said.

"Aye, aye, sir." Halfhyde looked at the hooded eyes, the jutting beard of Fitzsimmons. "Mr Runcorn deserts, I do not. Mr Runcorn, on his first voyage as a midshipman, has had enough."

"Off the Slave Coast, Mr Halfhyde?" Fitzsimmons raised formidable eyebrows.

"I am currently under orders to do the same in the same place, sir, am I not? And is not a midshipman less likely to be aware of the dangers, sir, than a lieutenant who has been there before?"

"Go on."

"So Mr Runcorn goes over the side with his baulk of timber, preferring even possible death to spending another moment aboard a British man-of-war. Or he could go involuntarily, as did poor Mr Lewis, perhaps. In any case, I go after him, intending rescue. We are not seen. The ship steams on. Is this not much more plausible, sir, than that I should desert?"

The Captain pulled at his beard, thinking deeply, a hand tapping on the open desk. There was a long silence, broken at last by Fitzsimmons calling for the marine sentry on duty outside the cabin. There was a crash of bootleather and the door opened. Woodenly, a face looked in with the steel of a bayonet shining alongside the right ear above the rifle in the shoulder-arms position. "Sir!"

"My messenger, with my compliments to Mr Runcorn. He is to come at once."

"I'll be damned thankful for your company, Wart," Halfhyde said as they walked the quarterdeck together, Mr Runcorn's short legs seeming to twinkle as they kept pace with Mr Halfhyde's long ones. "I'm grateful to you. Would you rather desert, or do a lubber's slide?"

The wart considered. "A lubber's slide, sir, if you please."

"Then a slide it shall be—the Captain has left that to us. You don't mind a reputation for wartish unhandiness, then?"

"It's better than being a *deserter,* sir!" The wart's voice was full of deep scorn. "I know I wouldn't *really* be one, sir, but . . ." His voice trailed away.

"You mean if things go wrong and can't be explained—your family?"

"Yes, sir. They were awf'lly proud, sir, when I entered."

"Following the tradition—Trafalgar?"

"Yes, sir."

"Well," Halfhyde said musingly, "you may be about to add more laurels. We'll not exactly be laid alongside the enemy, firing broad-sides into his decks and rigging—but we're undoubtedly going to need a touch of Nelson or I'm a Dutchman!"

Chapter 6

HMS *Aurora,* passing well to seaward of Cape Palmas, had turned easterly on Halfhyde's order to head for the Bight of Benin, maintaining a course that would keep her out of sight from the Ivory Coast. Halfhyde, after some hours of study of the charts and the Admiralty sailing directions for the area, had, on Fitzsimmons's order, taken over responsibility for the cruiser's navigation. Making good speed still, the *Aurora* closed what was to be her dropping position to the north-west of the mouth of the Benin river. From this dropping point the manned baulk of timber would be borne along the flow of water forming the counter-equatorial or Guinea current, which would also, in due time, carry Halfhyde and his companion on to the rendezvous position. This position had been agreed. The *Aurora* would cruise each day from dawn until noon in an area south-west of the Bight but well north of the point where the Guinea current was met and countered by the north-flowing Benguela current; she would have look-outs scanning the seas continuously for the returning officer and midshipman, who would rely upon Halfhyde's own knowledge of the local waters, and upon the boat's compass which he would have with him, for their navigation.

Fitzsimmons was on edge as his ship closed the tricky waters of the Bight. He stood on the bridge, lonely, uncommunicative, making much use of his telescope to ensure that he did not come within any sight from the shore, nose raised to sniff the unmistakable smell of the great African continent, a strange aroma composed of earth and spices and jungle vegetation that had indeed been wafted faintly towards them for many days now. Halfhyde, conning the cruiser in through well-remembered waters, sniffed the increasing smell appreciatively. Africa he had liked, even loved, in spite of all her undoubted dangers and discomforts. Currently, dangers, navigational ones, loomed already in the mind of Captain Fitzsimmons. Despite Halfhyde's assurances, backed by the chart, that there would be plenty of water to float the *Aurora* for as far as she needed to go, Fitzsimmons had ordered leadsmen into the chains to port and starboard. These men, brawny leading-seamen, time and again heaved the tallow-armed hand-leads, swinging the eight pound weights in great overarm circles to drop ahead of the cruiser's ram, all without finding bottom. Halfhyde shrugged, and grinned inwardly at Fitzsimmons's terrible caution, though he was forced to admit the naturalness of an urge for safety in an unknown area where the mud brought down by the outflow of the Benin and Escravos rivers could conceivably confound navigation unexpectedly.

Fitzsimmons came up, halted by his side. "Have a care, Mr Halfhyde."

"Aye, aye, sir. There's no need for anxiety."

"There is a very heavy ground swell, Mr Halfhyde, setting us towards the shore."

Halfhyde shrugged. "As ever, sir, as ever! Closer in, it increases, but we have no need to close the shore. You barely need a fix even . . . the water tells its own tale. The discolouration reaches out for some nine miles off shore—mud and scum, sir, as an advance warning. While the sea is clear, so is the ship." he added, "Meanwhile, sir, the ebb's running."

"How long had it been running, Mr Halfhyde?"

"Eight hours, sir."

"With a total run of nine hours?"

"Yes sir."

The Captain swung away and began a restless pacing of the bridge, back and forth. After a lengthy silence he stopped again. "Mr Halfhyde, where do you make our position now?"

Halfhyde left the standard compass and went towards the chart shelf just behind. He did some rapid pencil work, with parallel rulers and pointers, making a small neat cross on the chart. "There, sir, by dead reckoning from the noon sight . . . Fishtown bearing a hundred and ten degrees true, distant twenty-six miles."

"Then the telegraphs to slow ahead, Mr Halfhyde, and the Fleet Engineer to be told to give the minimum revolutions necessary to maintain steerage way, but to be ready instantly for more speed when ordered."

"Aye, aye, sir." Halfhyde repeated the order, which was passed to the engine-room by the Midshipman of the Watch. Thirty minutes later Fitzsimmons asked, "Mr Halfhyde, are we now in the current?"

Halfhyde nodded. "We are, sir, and close to flood tide as well."

"Then send for Mr Runcorn. Hands to stand by to jettison the timber."

Already in his imagination Halfhyde could hear the roar of surf from the distance.

• • •

The wart, too much on edge to do anything else, was in fact standing by the great baulk of timber lashed to a set of ring-bolts in the upper deck below Number One cutter. Shivering, he was waiting in the rig as ordered for his peculiar voyage: collarless shirt, and blue uniform trousers with half-Wellington leather boots. Halfhyde, who was to go overboard on his rescue mission dressed in uniform, found Runcorn watching a couple of seamen under a petty officer casting off the timber's lashings.

"Well, Wart, are you ready?"

Runcorn saluted. "Yes, sir."

"And eager?"

"Well, sir . . . yes, sir!"

Halfhyde grinned. "Wart, you're a bloody liar. I'm not eager, nor are you, but we'll not be downhearted, will we?"

"Oh no, sir!"

"Even though there's a change in the orders."

"Sir?"

"The Captain prefers after all to keep closer to the original instructions from the Board of Admiralty. I'm sorry, Mr Runcorn, but you are to desert."

"Oh, but sir!"

Halfhyde broke in harshly. "The Captain's order, Mr Runcorn. There is no more to be said. It's been said already, I assure you, but I must see the Captain's point, which is, that considering the intelligence awaiting the *Diadem's* captain in Gibraltar, too much change now would add a worse degree of confusion."

"Yes, sir."

"Good! Then what are you waiting for?"

"Sir?"

Halfhyde said testily, "Kindly *desert*, Mr Runcorn."

"Aye, aye, sir." The wart stepped to the side and looked down, more than a little fearfully. Moonlight was now slanting silver across the water, which, where the moonlight was not, was black as ink. Halfhyde gestured to the petty officer in charge of the timber-jettisoning party, who at once gave his orders. The baulk of timber was lifted to the guard-rail and pushed over. It went in with a smack and a cloud of spray, and the men watching from the deck saw it submerge for an instant and come up again, rolling over and over, looking oddly, and perhaps prophetically, like a crocodile.

"Over you go, Mr Runcorn."

The midshipman climbed the guard-rail and dived in. After him, a few seconds later, went St Vincent Halfhyde. Coming up, flinging water from his eyes and ears, he heard the shout from the upper deck to the bridge: "Party away, sir!"

Halfhyde, looking around in the moonlight saw that the wart had made the great piece of timber and was clinging to it. He swam towards him, taking it in leisurely fashion. There was no hurry. The water was warm, quite pleasant. As he reached the timber and its clinging figure, he heard a hail from the *Aurora's* navigating bridge. It was Fitzsimmons, using a megaphone. "Good luck, Mr Halfhyde. I shall be watching for you daily. Do your very best. Much depends upon you both."

Halfhyde decided not to waste breath and gave a wave. He heaved his body half clear of the water, draped himself across the timber, and gave the wart a hand up. The timber sogged down beneath their weight, well awash in the dark waters of the Gulf. Very slowly, almost infinitesimally slowly, the gap

widened between themselves and the cruiser. After some minutes they heard the sounds of life aboard, the clang of the
engine-room telegraph, then the thrash from aft as the main
shafts began turning the screws. In the moonlight, they saw the
cruiser swing, swing until her bows were pointing towards
them, then swing on and away to head out of the Gulf for open
sea. It was a lonely feeling, and for a while an uncomfortable
one. The timber rolled heavily as the wash from the outgoing
cruiser took them in what felt, in their lowly craft, like a giant's
hand. Mr Runcorn went under, and reappeared spluttering.

Halfhyde hauled the small form back aboard and said
solemnly, "You may speak your mind, Mr Runcorn, since you
have now deserted!"

Mr Runcorn spat water. "I haven't *really*, sir."

"Don't sound quite so desperately worried. I assure you, the
facts will be known in due course to the Admiralty. In the
meantime, allow me to be your mouthpiece." St Vincent
Halfhyde, rising dangerously upon the timber, shook a fist in
the direction of the retreating cruiser and her Captain. Strong
language rang out into the night as Halfhyde gave expression
to feelings perforce kept in bottle since leaving Portsmouth. The
wart looked amazed, as well he might, and Halfhyde, reaching
the end of inventiveness, laughed.

"Mr Runcorn," he said reflectively as they rode the swell, "I
realize you look upon the Captain as God—and by God, you're
right to do so! It's an attitude that captains like. I remember
when I stood my first foreign harbour watch as a lieutenant,
many years ago, I had the temerity to refuse a boat ashore for
the Fleet Paymaster, who reported the fact to my Captain,

though of course, as Officer of the Watch, I was within my rights—which my Captain was not slow to shout at the Fleet Paymaster. 'Paymaster,' he shouted, 'You have had the impertinence to question the word of God.' 'How so, sir?' the Paymaster asked. The Captain said, 'We are in a foreign port, thus I am the representative of Her Majesty the Queen. Her Majesty, as head of the Church of England, is God's representative upon earth. My Officer of the Watch represents me. Therefore, for the duration of his watch, he is to all intents and purposes God.'" Halfhyde laughed again. "Do you follow, Mr Runcorn?"

"Not really, sir. If that's the case, sir, then what you said about the Captain—"

"That's my point, Mr Runcorn. I'm not a very religious man. Blasphemy, for me, holds no terrors." St Vincent Halfhyde pulled his boat's compass from a lanyard around his neck. "Now, Mr Runcorn, we shall set a course as best we can for the Benin river—and may God protect us from the reptiles that lurk in it!" He laughed once more. "Religious or not, God's still my talisman!"

He realized that he had offended the wart's conventions.

The counter-equatorial current, moving at no more than one knot, aided if only a little the propulsive efforts of arms and legs. They rode the timber like swimming dogs, rushing down the swell to climb slowly to the next crest. The flood tide gave them extra assistance, pushing them on towards the land and the mouth of the Benin river. After some hours, the roar of the surf on the distant beach was loud, frightening, drowning all other sound as they drifted closer inshore. The smell of Africa was stronger now. As the dark came down again they were not far off the breakers. Beyond those breakers flickers of light were seen from time to time, the fires of fishermen, Halfhyde said.

"Yes, sir. There are more, sir—over there, sir. They seem higher, sir."

Halfhyde looked. Making a judgement against the flat background of the land and the trees behind the beach—land so flat that, had it been daylight, they would, even from a ship's bridge, have seen nothing until they had come within some four miles—he reckoned the lights to be above the water, a confusion of lights, coming clearer as they moved so slowly closer, lights with no pattern about them, lights that seemed to lift and fall again, heaving on the ground swell.

Halfhyde said, "It's the Russian squadron, Wart, rolling and pitching in the anchorage. It's what we've come for." He reached out a friendly hand. "Courage, boy, courage!" There was no response from the midshipman. They drifted on, in comparatively quiet water for the moment but close now to the first line of surf, and well into the scummy muck that floated on the surface and just below it, filth brought down on the ebb from the river mouths to linger and increase and to swill back towards the shore on the flood tide. It stank to heaven of all manner of rotting beastliness. Half swimming, thrusting from one side or the other so as to direct the course of the timber as best they could, they felt the flood tide take them more and more strongly landward. They remained unseen, for the moon had gone behind a vast cloud bank earlier and was still in hiding. They went on towards the line of surf breaking on the African beach, hearing its thunder, seeing its flung white spray luminous against the black of the trees. Just before the breakers took them, Halfhyde reached out again to the midshipman. "Heads just above the water," he said, shouting over the tremendous noise. "We're just a piece of driftwood, coming in on the rollers. Never mind the Board of Admiralty—I propose to meet Prince Gorsinski in *my* time, not his! All right?"

"Yes, sir."

"Take care, then, Wart. If you've never ridden surf before, you'll think you're drowning. Just cling on—that's all. I've learned the tricks from the natives. I'll get you through."

A moment later they were in. Swiftly they were seized, to be rushed up a sloping, moving wall of water to a breaking crest, a curling lash of sea creaming away to right and left before flinging them down into the trough. Going right beneath the gigantic wave, they seemed to remain submerged for an infinity of time, but gasping, with lungs bursting, they came through like drowned rats, eyes, ears and noses filled with water, all their senses battered by the terrible roar of the pounding surf. Never had Runcorn heard such a sound or suffered such violence to his body. He sped like a bullet down the next crest, parted now from the baulk of timber, which had rushed away below him on a strong surge of water. For a moment he saw Halfhyde's head farther inshore—a black dot against the white that quickly vanished in the darkness beneath a dropping, curling crest. Line after line after line of breakers, a torrential world of hurtling water, a body that felt as though it must surely fall apart, thunderous noise to fill the ears when the water left them, and then, like a blessed miracle, the mouth of the Benin river ahead as the wart's body was flung clear of the hard sandbar across the entrance. Inshore of the bar was comparative peace. There, too, Halfhyde, flat on his face on a sandy beach, tugged at by the violent undertow as some of the surf's force surged across the bar. Runcorn staggered towards the lieutenant and collapsed by his side.

Life came back. There was immense relief in the wart's face when Halfhyde stirred and spoke. "I'm all right now. Come along, Mr Runcorn, let's get clear of the undertow." He pulled himself to his feet, and gave Runcorn a hand up. Going slowly towards the trees fringing the beach, he looked seaward, back towards the Russian cruisers in the anchorage, some four to five miles from the river mouth, their lights still shining out as they surged to the swell. Halfhyde thought of Admiral Prince Gorsinski, perhaps dressing for dinner now, with that strange smell of Africa drifting in from along the Slave Coast, over his great stern-walk—Gorsinski, never dreaming of who was so clandestinely approaching the vicinity of his squadron. At that moment the earnest promises and assurances of Captain Fitzsimmons seemed to Halfhyde even less substantial than a whore's virginity.

Chapter 7

"WHERE are we, sir, exactly?"

Halfhyde waved a hand around. "On the beach, Mr Runcorn, on the Fishtown side of the river, in the territory of the Jekris."

"Jekris, sir?"

"One of the local tribes."

"Oh—yes, sir. Sir, the baulk of timber. It's gone, sir, some way out."

Halfhyde smiled. "Well, don't sound so sad, Wart, we'll not need it again. Come!" He continued up the beach towards the darkly-shrouded trees.

Following him, Runcorn was feeling nostalgic about the baulk of timber. The last lifeline had gone, the last link with the cruiser and with a retrospectively comforting naval routine. There was a looseness in Mr Runcorn's bowels as he looked at the jungle fringe behind the Benin river's sucking mud. In there dwelt more fearsome creatures, beast and man, than dwelt in the *Aurora's* distant gunroom.

Halfhyde, seeming to sense the direction of the midshipman's thoughts, placed a hand on his shoulder, giving it a strong grip of reassurance. "Never set foot on foreign soil before, Wart?"

"Not foreign, sir. The colonies, sir. A cruise, sir, to Gibraltar in the Training Squadron."

Halfhyde laughed. "A different kettle of fish from this place—

yet in a sense this is a colony, I suppose, at least to the extent that the National African Company has certain territorial rights here, as it has in the Coast Protectorates. Otherwise it is foreign enough, and open too—no formal colonial status, or we'd have the Russkies by the short hairs!"

Halfhyde delved into the waistband of his trousers and pulled out a heavy revolver in a tarred canvas cover. Unwrapping this, he held it close to his eyes and examined it, spinning the chambers. Mr Runcorn, who was similarly armed, checked his own weapon and asked, "Do we load, sir?"

"Yes, Mr Runcorn. If we wish to live, we load!" Halfhyde reached into a pocket and brought out cartridges wrapped in an oiled silk tobacco-pouch against the seawater. He slipped six rounds into the chambers. Ready now, the two moved ahead with the loaded revolvers in their hands.

Halfhyde said, "We'll not use them unless it's inevitable, Mr Runcorn."

"Aye, aye, sir."

"We must conserve our ammunition, and we must not alarm the Russians."

Halfhyde moved on up the beach, with Runcorn close behind, sweating freely now to add to the salt wetness and the smell of the clinging scum. There was a high humidity in this low-lying coastal strip, and it was unhealthy country, part of the territory known to exiled Europeans as the White Man's Grave, an area of yellow fever, malaria, blackwater fever, and many other terrible diseases that were largely killers. Soon, reaching the harder surface behind the beach, they came to the little township itself. They passed furtively along beside the shacks of the fishermen. Filthy as they were, they drew little attention. Perhaps the Jekris were accustomed to the sight of other white men, Russians, coming and going on expeditions up-country for shooting and hunting. There were few men about: they would be busy at the fishing. There were women and children around in the short twilight, women with skirts of grass or cloth supplied by the traders in return for work or favour, with large pendulant breasts sucked dry by clinging black babes in arms, or with withered, flattish appendages that dropped over the skirt-tops, folds of loose, empty, flesh, all charms worn away by age. Mr Midshipman Runcorn stared in horrified curiosity, looked away sharply and with a flushed face as one old crone opened a toothless mouth to grin at him when their eyes momentarily met.

"If one of them takes your fancy, Mr Runcorn," Halfhyde said gravely, "I've no doubt an assignation can be arranged in return for one of my shining brass buttons!"

The wart's response was shocked. "Oh, no, sir!"

"Oh, no, sir, indeed, when you are here for a short stay. Spare a thought for the deprivations suffered by the whites whose life's work lies along the Slave Coast, Mr Runcorn! There are times in an exile's life when a native girl is more than wel come!" They moved on. As they went past the entrance to a narrow, stinking lane to their left, Halfhyde seized the wart's arm and dragged him aside. "Russians!" he said. Before he was pushed into the alley's concealment, Runcorn had seen the two figures ahead, bluejackets carrying rifles with bayonets fixed. Halfhyde said, "I don't know if they've seen us, but we'll not chance it. Down the alley, as fast as you can."

They ran. At the end, Halfhyde looked back. "No chase," he said. "Better safe than sorry all the same, Wart."

"Yes, sir. Shall we go back the same way, sir?"

Halfhyde shook his head. "No, we'll go out this end, just in case." They moved out and came slap into the arms of another Russian, this time a whiskered officer in full uniform, complete with a gold-scabbarded sword. Speaking in fluent Russian, Halfhyde begged his pardon, apologizing elaborately. The officer took out a fine linen handkerchief and flapped at his sumptuous uniform, appearing disdainful of the two filthy figures who had accosted him, looking in astonishment at the mud-encrusted naval monkey-jacket worn by one of them. He drew his sword, pointing it at St Vincent Halfhyde.

"Who are you?" he asked harshly.

Halfhyde smiled, bowed, and then, very suddenly and rapidly, dived for the Russian's legs. He felt the sword-tip slice down his back, a thin trail of pain, then the Russian officer toppled. As Halfhyde swivelled clear, the heavy body fell with a crash. Halfhyde seized the sword-arm, twisting it back until the shoulder dislocated. He took up the sword as Mr Runcorn, at a word from him, stifled the cries of pain. "Into the alley with him," Halfhyde snapped. With one hand still clamped around the Russian's mouth, the midshipman assisted in the dragging. Halfhyde, breathing hard, feeling the blood from his spine soak into his sword-split uniform, laid the tip of the sword on the throat of the Russian officer, gently pricking at the adam's apple. Glancing at the midshipman, he saw the wince of pain on the boyish face.

"What's the matter, Mr Runcorn?" he asked.

"Sir, he is biting my hand."

Halfhyde pressed harder with the sword. "Let go, then. From you, my fine whiskery friend," he said in Russian, "no talking of any kind except in answer to my questions, the first of which is the name of your ship, if you please?"

There was no answer. Halfhyde drew a little blood with the sword, and the man writhed on the ground, his face wet with sweat that glistened in the last of the day's light. He said, "The *Romanov*."

"The flagship, eh?" Halfhyde smiled. "And Admiral Prince Gorsinski? Why is he here in the Bight of Benin?"

The Russian gathered saliva in his mouth, brought his head up, and spat. The result struck Halfhyde's trousers, and drooled down. The Russian said, "My admiral's intentions are his concern, not yours. Who are you? Where do you come from?"

Halfhyde paused, looking down at the man on the ground, in the filth of the native alley. He had been too impetuous. He removed the point of the sword from the Russian's throat and stood back, smiling. He bowed. Still speaking in Russian, he said, "Pray accept my apologies, sir. A case of mistaken identity, I assure you. But you would be unwise to ask questions all the same, for I might decide to kill you." He transferred the sword to his left hand, and with his right brought out his revolver, aiming it at the Russian's chest. "If you go now, peacefully, you go with a whole skin."

The Russian glowered. "My sword?"

"You'll have it back. Your word that you will turn and go?"

"You have it. My sword, I say."

Halfhyde handed the hilt to the Russian officer, who took it. Remarking that his assailants had by no means heard the last of their attack, he carried out a retreat with such dignity as he had been left with. Scowling, Halfhyde watched him go. Runcorn asked, "Sir, what shall we do now?"

"Run like the devil," Halfhyde snapped, turning back the way they had come and setting the pace. At the end of the alley, he slowed and halted just inside, looking carefully round the angle of a shack before beckoning the midshipman out. "Keep your eyes open," he said. "We'll not run now—not unless we have to, that is!"

They walked on fast. Runcorn said, "That Russian, sir. Wouldn't it have been better to have killed him, sir?"

Halfhyde gave a short laugh. "Why, damn it all, Mr Runcorn, for a wart you're too bloodthirsty by half! We are not *at war* with Russia, and frankly I've no wish to be charged with murder."

"No sir." Runcorn hesitated. "Sir, I heard you mention the name of Prince Gorsinski to the Russian. I was wondering? . . ."

"Are you," Halfhyde snapped, "about to offer more criticism, Mr Runcorn?"

"Oh, no, sir!"

"Just as well. You will kindly shut your mouth from now on."

"Yes, sir." The wart leapt a foot in the air as a high, hoarse screeching noise came from close at hand. "Sir, what was that?"

"Guinea-fowl," Halfhyde said irritably. "You'll get used to it." They went on, Halfhyde looking as bitter as gall. He was conscious of a situation mishandled from the start, and dangerously so. He sniffed the air. There was, he fancied, a hint of the rains to come. They were well into March now, and March normally brought in the wet season; so far, he judged, there had been little beyond the customary isolated downpours that heralded the worse to come. At the end of the rough, pitted track between the shacks of the Jekris, they came within sight of the banks of the Benin river again, around the corner as it were from the open sea. Here, in the comparatively quiet waters of the river, was a rough wooden jetty outlined by a storm lantern. In the light of another lantern, the watchers saw the golden glint of an officer's epaulettes moving along the planks. A moment later, the gold vanished as an oilskin and sou'-wester were donned.

"For my money," Halfhyde said, "that's our friend."

"Yes, sir. Will there be a boat waiting, sir, do you suppose?"

"Not a ship's boat. He'll go out in a native canoe, with a native crew, and meet a ship's boat lying off to seaward of the surf." Harshly, Halfhyde laughed. "An uncomfortable trip, and I hope he doesn't survive it, though I fear he will. Within the next hour or so he'll be reporting to Prince Gorsinski. I've been a fool—and by God I admit it!"

The wart maintained a discreet silence.

"Come," Halfhyde said, swinging away from the prospect of the river. "We have shelter in view—for a time, anyway."

Music came from the house, weird native music of thin, reedy pipes and a monotonous, flat drumbeat. That, and raised voices, and now and then laughter. The house itself stood out among the poor dwellings of Fishtown almost like a baronial hall amid its clustered cots. Though built chiefly of wood, it had a solid look, and was of two storeys with a verandah and a balcony over it. From windows giving on to this balcony, dim light flickered eerily.

Halfhyde, with the midshipman beside him, knocked at a side door. There was no answer. He knocked again, harder, a peremptory thundering of a fist on thick wood. The door opened fractionally, and a shining black face was seen.

Halfhyde said, "Senhora da Luz, at once."

"Who wants the Senhora?"

"I do," Halfhyde answered with a harsh laugh. "Get her, and let me in, if you value your life." He put his foot in the door, which was about to close. Thrusting with his shoulder, he sent it inwards and stepped into a passage lit at its far end by a smoking oil lamp set in a bracket on a dirty wall of flaking plaster. The black man vanished, scuttling through a curtain of beads a little way beyond the light. Halfhyde gestured to Runcorn to shut the outer door.

"What is this place, sir?" Runcorn asked.

Halfhyde laughed. "You don't know, lad? Have a guess!"

"A bar, sir?"

"A bar certainly, but other things also. A useful rendezvous for seafarers, Mr Runcorn, as you shall discover, and run by a good friend of mine from days long past." He stopped speaking as the bead curtain parted and an immense brown-faced women came through, wearing a long black dress and many strings of pearls cascading down an out-thrust bosom. Runcorn stared in fascination. Never had he seen such a monstrous looking woman, so large and raddled a face haloed by such a profusion of childlike ringlets of the deepest black.

The woman stopped stock still at the sight of Halfhyde. She opened her mouth wide in evident astonishment and pleasure, then flung her thick puffy arms in the air. "Senhor Halfhyde! It is really you? You have come back to Fishtown and your Bella?"

Halfhyde bowed. "I have indeed, but—incognito. Your voice is loud, Senhora—"

"But I am so happy . . . so happy to see you!" She advanced, enfolded Halfhyde in her arms despite his appalling smell, and kissed him. Halfhyde extricated himself, and patted her on the shoulder. Mr Runcorn, looking on in wonder and some embarrassment, saw the sparkle of tears in the immense woman's eyes.

"I come to ask your help," Halfhyde said abruptly.

"My help, Senhor?"

"You were a good friend when I was last in Fishtown. My one friend on the Slave Coast. I think you are still that, Bella."

She clasped fat hands. "Oh, I am!"

"Good! Then you will give me shelter—and my young friend?" Turning, Halfhyde beckoned to the midshipman. "Come here, Wart, and be introduced to a great lady. Senhora, this is Mr Runcorn, a midshipman of the British Fleet. Mr Runcorn, Senhora da Luz, from Brazil."

Senhora da Luz held out a hand; bashfully, the wart took it, lifted it to his lips. Halfhyde laughed. "Beautifully done, Mr Midshipman Runcorn, very nicely in the tradition of Lord Charles Runcorn of Trafalgar!"

He turned back to Senhora da Luz. "Time is short," he said. "Explanations later, if you don't mind, my dear. It's not just food and soap and lodging we want—we want a safe place to hide, and that quickly!"

The Brazilian woman looked anxious. "Hide from whom, Senhor?"

"The Russians." Briefly, Halfhyde told her about the Russian officer. "I'm not unaware of the dangers, Bella. At a word from you, we'll leave. I've no wish to get you into the Russians' bad books, but, on the other hand, your house always had a certain . . . sanctity, if I may use the word, in the old times."

"As to that," the Senhora said at once, "there is no change."

Halfhyde lifted an eyebrow. "Prince Gorsinski?"

"And his captains, Senhor Halfhyde. Prince Gorsinski has been but two days in Fishtown, but my house is widely known, and His Highness has—"

"Availed himself of his opportunities—I guessed as much!" Halfhyde relaxed. "Nevertheless, there will be questioning before long—so if you please, Senhora, the safe hiding-place quickly!"

The hiding-place, though safe enough provided its occupants kept dead still from time to time, was thoroughly uncomfortable and constricted. It lay in the pitch-black space between the floor of the top storey and the ceiling of the downstairs apartments, in that section that lay over Senhora da Luz's private drawing-room. When the Russians came, as come they did within the hour in the person of an officer with a party of seamen, the voices could be heard with a fair degree of clarity. Lying motionless with an ear to the ceiling beneath his outstretched body, Halfhyde listened to Senhora da Luz dealing forcefully with her inquisitors. No persons of the given description had been in or near her establishment. She was positive on the point. Yes, she would pass the word if such should visit her bar, since she had no wish to lay herself open danger from desperadoes, or to rowdyism, or indeed to displease Prince Gorsinski. But no, she declared loudly, she would permit no search of her premises, none whatever. Her customers valued their privacy and relied upon her, Senhora Bella da Luz, to guard it with her very life. If the officer persisted in carrying out a search without her permission, then she would personally inform Prince Gorsinski, who, for reasons of his own, would be far from pleased.

The sounds of the voices diminished, then faded altogether. Halfhyde sighed with relief, and transferred his attention to other sounds coming from above: footfalls, soft laughter, shoes being kicked off, then the rythmic creaking of a bed. When this, too, ceased, and the closing of a door was heard above, Halfhyde felt the wart's hand on his shoulder.

"Yes?" he whispered.

"Sir, I believe it's a bedroom above us."

"Naturally."

There was a pause, then again the low whisper: "I really think this place is a—a *brothel, sir.*"

Indiscreetly, Halfhyde gave a laugh, quickly smothered. A few minutes later the trapdoor through which they had come, opened, and the lowered face of Senhora da Luz was seen in flickering lamplight. "Come," she said. They scrambled out, dust-covered and stiff. The trapdoor, set into the wall of a small closet, was nicely concealed behind a row of hanging garments smelling of mothballs. The senhora led them down the stairs to her drawing-room, an ornately-furnished apartment containing heavy armchairs with lace antimacassars, mosquito netting over door and windows, and a parrot, green and blue and yellow, angrily scattering seed from a hanging cage. From one of the chairs a young girl rose, a girl of such great beauty that it made Halfhyde gasp for a moment.

"This is Dolores," Senhora da Luz said, smiling. "You remember her—my little daughter?"

"I'll be damned!" Halfhyde said in astonishment. "She was a child when I was last here . . . now she's a damn raving beauty, and a grown woman too!" He crossed the room with long strides and took her hand, raising it to his lips and feeling the hot blood strongly pumping as he did so. Then, clamping control upon himself, he turned away and introduced Mr Midshipman Runcorn. The girl, tall and slim, black-haired as naturally as her mother was dyed, and with large, almost violet eyes, was polite but distant to Mr Runcorn. Halfhyde's pulse raced: in the instant of meeting, he had felt the unmistakable, quickened interest, the involuntary response. There was something electric between them, something that could not be disregarded by any strong man to whom little love had come, but there was something also that stood sentinel. Bella da Luz, once Halfhyde's mistress, clearly expected to be so still; and Halfhyde hadn't the heart to disappoint her.

At 2 A.M. St Vincent Halfhyde gave a sigh, a very heart-felt one indeed. He was spent, and Bella was still urgent. The years, he reflected bitterly, had brought a sad and rather frightening change. Once, Senhora da Luz, of no particular husband despite the *senhora,* had closely resembled the shape, the present shape, of her distracting daughter—but, alas, no longer. Where there had been clawing muscle, there was now flab; where strongly-clasping legs, more sagging flesh to blanket and constrict desire. Her breath came hot, but also aromatic. St Vincent Halfhyde had had the very devil of a job to display any evidence of desire at all, and had managed it only by means of intense concentration upon his mental image of Dolores, currently in her virginal bed. The fact that this was where she was gave Halfhyde his only balm. She had been high and mighty towards Mr Runcorn while for his part the wart had appeared as terrified of her as he was of Mr Dalrymple-Martin, sub of a very distant, sea-keeping gunroom. Thinking of the wart's bashfulness before beauty, Halfhyde grinned. By the time they rejoined the *Aurora,* Mr Runcorn, in one way or another, might very well have lost his own virginity. What better training-ground for a midshipman than within the very portals of a first-class—by Slave Coast standards—brothel? Bella da Luz had a reputation to think of, and she was mightily particular. All her girls were young, and all were white: South Americans mainly, some Spanish, some French. A wart's paradise.

St Vincent Halfhyde sighed again, and turned back to his undoubted duty. Bella had to be kept sweet in the interests of Her Majesty, who would no doubt be most surprised to learn of the varied ways in which she was served in the distant parts of the world.

At half past three that morning, when the house was otherwise very quiet, there came a thunderous knocking on the door of the bar, accompanied by the rattle of rifles and bayonets.

Chapter 8

BEFORE that knocking had come, Halfhyde had turned the night to some good account at least. Bella da Luz was, as ever in the past, a fine source of information, and now she it was who gave him his cue.

"The Russians, my love . . ."

"Yes, Bella?"

"From your story, you will have offended them badly, I think?"

"An understatement. They'll be out for blood, Bella. I've met Prince Gorsinski before." He told her, briefly, of the circumstances. On his last visit to Fishtown, he had not revealed his earlier captivity. Now, it was more than germane. "An unfortunate set of circumstances has brought us together again. I'm going to need my wits about me, I can tell you that!"

"Why," she asked in a puzzled voice, "are you here? You speak of your Master Runcorn being a deserter from your ship, but somehow I do not believe this."

"You don't? Why not?"

"Oh, I do not know why not, my love." She wriggled in his arms, a mountain shivering to internal eruptions. "It is just a feeling. An officer—"

"A makee-learn officer only, Bella."

"Yet with the fine future of an officer in the British Fleet. And he is so innocent! Butter would not melt in his mouth!"

"We can change that, you and I," Halfhyde said with a low laugh, "though I fear his mother would hardly approve! Innocent he may be, and basically decent he is without a doubt. But you, Bella, you've not lived in a gunroom. This was his first voyage as a midshipman, remember, and he found it too much to bear. The bullying would surprise you, Bella."

"I have heard about it," she said, wriggling again. "Has it been worse for Master Runcorn, than for others like him?"

"Much worse," Halfhyde said, fondling her breasts from a sense of obligation. "The *Au*—the *Diadem*, Bella, is a hard ship, with hard officers brought up in the old Navy under sail. Warts are treated as less than human. Mastheadings, floggings and so on—on the official plane, that is. Unofficial beatings in the gunroom—a life of near torture, with no one to listen to complaints. It has broken many young men of spirit, Bella."

"Yet you behaved with compassion, my love?"

"Me?"

"You dived to his rescue, and that was very brave."

"Oh, no," Halfhyde said modestly. "Not brave. Just a duty reflex, that's all. He had to be brought back. The trouble was, neither of us *were*, thanks to a damned blind fool of an Officer of the Watch, and look-outs who shall face court martial when we rejoin the Fleet!"

"You are the young man's gaoler, then, my love?"

"In a sense, yes. I must take him back to England, or to the Cape perhaps, aboard any British ship that enters. In the meantime . . . my curiosity is aroused by the Russian ships, Bella. What are they doing here, d'you know?"

"Bringing trade," Senhora da Luz said with a giggle. "Much trade!"

"For you, yes, I understand that, but trade in general terms rather than particular—is there evidence of this, Bella?"

Her lips brushed against his ear. She was tiring of the business of question and answer. "There are new trading posts here in Fishtown, yes."

"Russian?"

"Yes. Important men came in the first ship to arrive, the *Grand Duke Alexis,* some weeks ago. My love, I—"

"How have the Russians behaved, Bella?"

"Very well, so far as I am concerned."

"And the rest of Fishtown?"

She said, "I think there is anxiety. The traders, mostly Portuguese . . . they prefer the British. They fear for their livelihoods, which are already much affected since the trading is done only with the Russians."

"No contact with other visiting ships?" Halfhyde asked, remembering what he had been told at the Admiralty.

Bella nodded. "Yes, that is so, no other sailors have been allowed to land, the jetty has been guarded by armed sentries, and boats patrol between the shore and the ships that enter. But the traders fear also the reasons for the building of a fort of big guns, which the Russians have placed behind the town."

"Do they fear anything else, Bella?"

He was conscious of her sudden inhalation. "I do not know, my love, my dearest. I do not know of anything—"

"There've been no . . . disappearances, sudden, perhaps, and unexplained?"

It was at that moment that the knocking came from below; the question remained unanswered. Halfhyde, fleetingly registering that Bella had sounded as if she wouldn't have answered in any case, was out of bed in a bound. Crouching by the window, he lifted a corner of the curtain behind the mosquito net. Since the window gave on to the balcony he could see nothing but the fringe of a pool of light, probably coming from a storm lantern. He heard vague sounds, the clink of rifles and equipment, the shuffle of booted feet, then the second tattoo on the bar door. He went across the room by touch, in pitch darkness, found the chair over which he had thrown his clothing, and quickly pulled on shirt and trousers. He went back to Bella, who was sitting up in bed, her huge body taut with anxiety as he put out a hand to her.

"I'm going," he said, "and taking the wart with me."

"No, no!"

"I'll not risk bringing trouble to you, Bella. You've been a good friend." Bending, he kissed her. Her face felt cold as a wobbling blancmange. He said, "Give me two minutes. Then go down and open up to them."

"You will never get away," she said fearfully. "The back will be watched, the house surrounded; it will be the worse for me, my love."

"There's truth in that," Halfhyde said, frowning. "All right, then! Two of your girls, Bella, any that are free. Tell me where to go."

The two rooms at the end of the passage outside," Senhora da Luz said. "The girls' names . . . there is Maria and—"

"Right!" Halfhyde was already moving for the door. "Two minutes, Bella."

He went out. On the landing an oil lamp was burning, its wick turned low. Taking it from its bracket, Halfhyde ran along the passage, stopped at the door of the room where the midshipman was sleeping, and went in at the rush, calling Runcorn's name urgently. There was a scuffle from the bed and Runcorn sat up, obviously doing his best to conceal the body of a young woman.

"Sir," he said, sounding acutely embarrassed.

Halfhyde, amused despite the danger stifled a shout of rising laughter. There was pathos in the interruption of a young man's first exercise in womanizing. "By God, Wart, you're doing fine! Just carry on—and don't sound so damn shy, it's perfectly natural. Didn't you hear the knocking?"

"Oh yes, sir, but—"

"All right. When they come, we're just plain customers. Remember your story and give it in full, but no involvement of Senhora da Luz. We just turned up on her, that's all—she doesn't know me. All right, Mr Runcorn?"

"Yes, sir!"

Halfhyde went out, shutting the door behind him, and ran to the last room off the passage. He flung the door open. In the bed a young girl sat up, staring. Halfhyde tore off his clothes and snapped, "You have a customer, Maria."

"I am Yvette—"

"Don't split hairs; you've still got a customer. And if you value the life of your good senhora, and perhaps your own too, I've been in your bed since 11 PM." Stripped naked, Halfhyde thumped into the bed beside her and took her in his arms. The knocking, added to now by angry and impatient shouts, continued.

The Russian officer, who was not the one Halfhyde and Runcorn had encountered earlier, ripped back Mr Runcorn's bedclothes, looked down with glittering eyes at naked flesh, and laughed loudly.

"A boy, fresh from the nursery," he said in Russian to his patrol. There was increased laughter, which added to the wart's terrible embarrassment.

"I beg your pardon?" he said.

The officer stared. "English?"

"Yes, sir, I am English. Do you speak English?"

"Small English I speak, yes. I wish an account from you, please."

"An account, sir? An account of what, sir?"

The Russian guffawed. He was young but hairy, with a coarse, heavy face, and thick lips. "Of your prowess, my little one, your prowess with the woman."

The wart flushed scarlet, his mouth opening and shutting like a landed fish. The girl, as naked as he, gave the Russian a reproachful look, and nuzzled her cheek against the wart's, murmuring words of comfort in halting English. The Russian's eyes narrowed, his mouth hardened: the time for pleasantries was over. He reached for the girl, seizing her by one arm and yanking her bodily from the bed to send her flinging across the room to the farther wall, where she landed in a heap, crying. At that, the wart stood up.

"Sir," he said, his eyes flashing fire. "Sir, you'll not do that to a lady—"

"You will stop me, perhaps, English child?"

"I'm no child, sir!"

"Who are you? Tell me, or I put out your eyes."

The wart stared. The officer had lifted his sword, and the point was towards his right eye, no more than two inches away. The wart, who had heard stories of Russian barbarities, swallowed hard and felt his very guts melt away. The man looked capable enough of carrying out his threat, and anyway, his own lieutenant's orders were clear enough. Mr Runcorn cleared his throat of his fear and drew himself up as proudly as was possible in a naked state.

"My name, sir, is Edward Perceval Standish Runcorn, and I am a midshipman in Her Britannic Majesty's fleet."

"The British Fleet?" The officer, clearly astonished, looked round momentarily at the men of his patrol. "I see no British ship in the bay. How is this, I ask?"

Runcorn said, "My ship is not here, sir. My ship—"

"What ship?"

"Her Majesty's cruiser Diadem, from the Cape to the Medway, to join the Nore command after she has refitted at Chatham, sir."

"And you?"

The wart's face was stony with the shame of the lie he had to tell. Though not meeting the Russian's eye, he told his story manfully. "I have deserted from my ship, sir, while she was off the Gulf. I took some timber with me . . . and the current brought me in."

In the silence that followed, he grew more scarlet, and then broke the silence by adding, "I claim the right to be treated as an officer and a gentleman, sir. I am here in this house by right, as a free Englishman, and you have no cause to interfere with me."

"A deserter, who claims the rights of an officer?" The Russian laughed again. "Such talk is—"

"I am still officially a midshipman of the British Fleet, sir, borne on the books of HMS Diadem, as you will find to your cost if there is ill-treatment."

The Russian sneered. "Fine words, but not impressive." He

turned to his armed sailors. "He is one we want," he said in his own language. "Take him."

Two men stepped forward and roughly seized the wart's arms, twisting them up behind his back until he winced with pain. He gasped, "Where are you taking me?"

"You will see." The Russian gave another order. Still naked, Mr Runcorn was marched out of the room, along the passage, and down the stairs. At the bottom was St Vincent Halfhyde, also naked, also held by the arms. Halfhyde smiled, and called out, "Chin up, Mr Runcorn—" He broke off sharply as a bayonet, pushed into a thigh, drew blood that ran down his leg to his ankle. He stared boldly at the man who had used the bayonet. In English he said, "You are a pond of excreta, my friend, and given time you will be made to sink within yourself." He looked at the wart again. "Courage, boy, courage. We're not lost yet." He raised his voice in a shout: *"Rule Britannia!"*

Leaving the house under strong escort, they heard the cries of women. Looking sideways at Halfhyde, the midshipman saw the way in which the lieutenant's mouth tightened, saw white teeth bite into the lower lip, and blood run down the chin. Halfhyde's mind was tumultuous, bitter. He brought no luck to anybody. Senhora da Luz, in her interrogation by the Russian officer who had remained behind, would have no cause to love him further. Halfhyde would have given much to have spared her, but it was no use harking back to what was done. The future had now to be faced manfully, and turned to such good account as was possible. At least Prince Gorsinski was a gentleman, an aristocrat. In that, perhaps, lay Halfhyde's only hope, and poor Runcorn's too. More bitter thoughts. It was his responsibility, and his alone, that the wart had been dragged into this. If anything went wrong, a mother, fondly from a distance regarding a son's first voyage to foreign parts, would have no kind thoughts for Halfhyde when the telegram came from the Board of Admiralty. But better not to think of that! Halfhyde, turning his mind with an effort to other things as his bare feet trod the filth of the Fishtown waterfront towards the wooden planks of the jetty, reflected on the better aspects. The *Aurora,* cruising on her station outside the Gulf of Guinea, with her potential landing-parties of armed seamen, and her marines, and her big guns, was Halfhyde's sheet anchor. Yet a very distant one, and one that could not be contacted. It was wholly up to Captain Fitzsimmons to ponder, to interpret, to assess. If Captain Fitzsimmons made a wrong assessment, if Captain Fitzsimmons played a safe hand and remained distant, no blame would ever attach to himself. Lieutenant St Vincent Halfhyde could be a very useful scapegoat, and could scarcely be said to stand high in the favour of Fitzsimmons, or of the Admiralty either. Halfhyde scowled. One bitter thought led to another, an unbreakable chain of woe and depression. There was yet another. Halfhyde, a sentimental and patriotic man deep inside though it seldom showed too overtly, and never mind Dr Johnson, would swell with pride in his race and his profession if he were allowed the sight of HMS *Aurora* steaming magnificently in through the mudbanks of the Bight of Benin, with leadsmen in the chains and her guns manned for action, the Battle Ensign flying large from the main topmast. But with no less then three ships of a heavy Russian squadron waiting for her, the result must be a foregone conclusion.

Chapter 9

IT was a nightmare trip, far worse than the inward passage on the baulk of timber, though the native crews were skilful and adroit. Halfhyde went in one canoe, Runcorn in another, with the native fishermen and a strong Russian guard in each. They flung through the breakers, to be half drowned in seconds, almost hurled from the flimsy craft as the bows lifted to the rollers, coming practically up-and-down as they burst through the crests. Behind the surf, in calmer but still restless swollen seas, cold and miserable, they were transferred to a ship's cutter from the *Romanov*, and brought alongside the heaving Russian flagship. One ship was much like another. But for certain differences, Halfhyde could have fancied himself boarding a British ship as he was pushed ahead of the bayonets up the quarter-deck ladder of the *Romanov*. Of those differences one was tangible, the other intangible. The Russian flagship was not as spotlessly clean as a British warship would be, and the overall atmosphere held a subtle distinction, one that Halfhyde had been much aware of when in Russian hands in Sevastopol: the cleavage between officers and men was virtually total. The British Navy had never been noted for any marked tendency towards democracy, indeed by its very nature a ship was, and had to be, an autocracy, with the captain the fount of all power and decision. But the British Navy, except in isolated cases, was not a despotism, and this was. Halfhyde, as he and Runcorn stepped upon the quarterdeck and came below the awning, was very conscious of a kind of cringing fear on the part of the seaman in the presence of their officers, a fear that was laced by something that should have penetrated the cold indifference of the Russian ruling class and caused them also to fear: a violent but as yet only smouldering hatred. To St Vincent Halfhyde, accustomed to a different mould of seaman, it was obvious in the guarded looks in the lean, somewhat hungry faces of the men at the head of the accommodation-ladder, in their stance, in the withdrawn manner of their speaking as orders were thrown to them as to dogs. Halfhyde thought back to his long year of imprisonment. The atmosphere was sharper now, more clear-cut.

With a close escort of armed sailors, he and the midshipman were taken below, clattering down steel ladders into the sweaty stench of tropical mess decks. It was the smell of hundreds of bodies pouring their sweat into bedding in enclosed spaces that little fresh air ever permeated, except during periods at sea in calm waters, when the wind-scoops could be fitted to the ports to catch any breath of breeze made by the ship's passage. They were pushed along narrow night darkened alleyways, again closely resembling the lower-deck lay-out of any British warship. They were taken right forward, and down to another deck, to where the space narrowed to right and left as the ship's side closed in towards the *Romanov's* great phosphor-bronze ram before the bow. Here, in the space just aft of the starboard cable locker, they were halted by another seaman carrying a bunch of keys. This man flung open the doors of adjoining cells. Halfhyde and Runcorn were pushed into seperate compartments, and the steel doors were banged to and securely locked. Looking through a small round aperture set in the door at about chest height, Halfhyde met a cold Russian eye staring back at him. During the remainder of the night he listened to the slither of the sentry as the ship rolled to the swell, and to the occasional bang of a rifle-butt on steel decking. Sitting on a steel bed-shelf as naked as his own body, Halfhyde gave himself up to gloomy introspection. Nobody could have handled this affair worse.

There was no port in the cell, no changing light-pattern against which to check the time. Outside the police-lights continued to burn, visible through the tiny inspection hole. As time slowly passed, bugle calls were heard, rousing the ship's company. Soon the decks came alive.

Later, Halfhyde heard footsteps approaching his cell, and there was some low conversation outside, preceded by a smart rattle of equipment and a bang of feet as the sentry saluted.

Once again Halfhyde peered through the hole. He saw gold lace and aigulettes. He braced himself. Those gilded ropes and tassels indicated Prince Gorsinski's Flag Lieutenant. A moment later, the key went into the lock and the door was opened up. The Flag Lieutenant, tall and slim, head held back and upper lip curling, surveyed him from head to foot.

"You are the man Halfhyde," the Russian said in his own language.

Halfhyde looked back coolly, maintaining his dignity, he hoped, despite the basic disadvantage of total nudity. He said,

"I am Lieutenant St Vincent Halfhyde, Royal Navy. I—"

"Silence!" The Flag Lieutenant addressed the sentry without looking at him. "You."

The sentry saluted. "Sir?"

"Clothing for the Englishman. Bring some."

"Sir, my orders—"

"Go. I am giving you the orders. If you speak again, the cat-o'-nine-tails waits. I shall guard the prisoner."

The man turned away smartly with his rifle and marched off. The Flag Lieutenant who had drawn a revolver, pointed it at Halfhyde's chest. "You are to be interviewed by the Admiral himself," he said. "I advise you to speak the truth, Lieutenant Halfhyde."

"Certainly I shall do that, but I must point out that the British Government will be asking some very searching questions of—"

"Silence! It is not for you to speak until you are questioned, and I am not interested in your British Government, Lieutenant Halfhyde, nor, you will find, is Prince Gorsinski."

Halfhyde shrugged. "Be it on your own heads, then—you *and* Prince Gorsinski!"

With no change in his cold expression, the Flag Lieutenant leaned slightly forward and brought the back of his hand across Halfhyde's cheek, hard. He was wearing a heavy gold ring which cut the flesh, and blood ran down Halfhyde's chin. Halfhyde remained motionless, smiling to cover his mounting rage, like an inferno inside him. He wanted nothing so much as to smash a fist into this gilded popinjay's arrogant mouth. His one attack was a passive one. He stared the Russian out, and was rewarded by a look of baffled fury before the eyes turned away. One day, he promised himself, before he rejoined the *Aurora,* he would meet the Flag Lieutenant without the intermediary of a well-aimed revolver.

The sentry was back within five minutes, bearing a uniform suit of plain white duck with a broad, deep collar hanging down its back. This the Flag Lieutenant regarded disdainfully, ordering it to be thrown towards Halfhyde. "Dress," he ordered.

Halfhyde looked down at the white duck, then up at the officer. "Am I to be dressed in rating's gear?" he asked. "May I remind you of my—"

"Dress, Lieutenant Halfhyde, or you will also be flogged as a rating—as a common seaman. Consider yourself lucky to be given clothing of any kind. This you owe to the fact that the Admiral, a fastidious man, cannot be presented with your offensive nakedness!" He moved his revolver closer to Halfhyde. "Pick it up, and dress—at once!"

Shrugging, fighting down his burning rage, Halfhyde did so. Dressed, he in fact felt better, more in control of himself. He asked, "And Mr Runcorn? Is he to accompany—"

"He will be questioned separarely from you. Now come." The Flag Lieutenant gestured with his revolver. "Aft, up the ladder and along the alleyway. You will keep walking and you will not turn round. If you do not obey, I shall shoot."

Barefoot, Halfhyde started aft, coming back again into the slippery, rolling mess decks, where the men, under their petty officers, were engaged in clearing away their bedding. As the prisoner and escort passed along, work stopped on the petty officers' shouted commands, and the men came to attention for the Flag Lieutenant. Halfhyde, noting the strange absence of any curiosity, felt again the bitter loathing for the afterguard so evident in the closed, impassive faces. It was an almost unnerving feeling, to be isolated in the midst of so much ill-will, in a situation that held so much explosive danger below the hatch-covers of bloodyhanded despotism, and Halfhyde was conscious of a sense of relief and almost freedom as he stepped from the ladder rising to the quarterdeck. This feeling was not due to last. Directed towards a hatchway aft of a turretted gun, he enjoyed fresh air and a sight of the thick green of the jungle stretching away behind Fishtown's five-mile-distant waterfront for no more than half a minute before he was once again below decks, though this time in a very different setting. Austerity, the austerity inseparable from warship life, was here muted and softened by the promise of luxury. The decks were clean, the bulkheads freshly painted, the brasswork gleaming with much human endeavour. There was quiet also, only their own footfalls breaking the silence as they approached the Admiral's quarters in the stern. Outside the Admiral's door a sentry came to attention, staring woodenly over the officer's head. Disregarding the man, the Flag Lieutenant told Halfhyde to open the door. They entered a small lobby with three more doors opening off: day cabin, sleeping cabin, bathroom. Coming up alongside Halfhyde, the Flag Lieutenant tapped on the heavy mahogany of the day cabin door, and was bidden to enter.

Halfhyde stepped into a luxurious cabin, a large apartment with three square ports opening on to the stern walk. At a roll-top desk similar to Fitzsimmons's, sat Prince Gorsinski, a powerful man with a heavy square face, thickly bearded, with wiry black hair slightly greying over the prominent ears. Large, rather luminous eyes surveyed Halfhyde for a while, in a heavy silence. Then Gorsinski nodded dismissingly at the Flag

Lieutenant, who snapped his heels together, bowed, and left the cabin.

"Mr Midshipman Halfhyde," Gorsinski said in a low voice, "returns himself to my custody at last!"

Halfhyde bowed. "Lieutenant Halfhyde now, Your Highness."

"So I am told. My congratulations."

"Thank you, sir." Halfhyde gave a cough. "I must disagree on another point, with respect, sir."

Gorsinski lifted thick eyebrows. "How so?"

"I am not returning myself to your custody. I have not even come aboard willingly, sir. With my midshipman, I have been, it appears, arrested. Or, as some would say, shanghaied."

"Who would say this, do you suppose?"

Halfhyde shrugged. "The British Admiralty. Even perhaps Her Majesty, who—"

"Her Majesty, your Queen Victoria, is a bumptious old woman who says very many things to very many people. But do I understand you to threaten me, Lieutenant Halfhyde?"

"By God you do, sir," Halfhyde said with a laugh. "I am a British naval officer—"

"Who attacked one of my lieutenants in Fishtown, and before that escaped whilst a prisoner."

"You cannot hold me or Mr Runcorn, sir. You have not the right."

"Right? What is right, Lieutenant Halfhyde?" Prince Gorsinski rose to his feet, thick, straight-backed, as tough as a gorilla. "Allow me to tell you what is right. Right is power—and I have the power! I imagine you will not deny this?"

Halfhyde shook his head. "No, I don't deny it, sir. But the power is temporary only. When word reaches Whitehall that

Mr Runcorn and I are held aboard your flagship, then a fleet will be despatched to the Bight of Benin to—"

"To cut you out?" Gorsinski gave a deep bellow of laughter. "I think not! Come, my dear fellow, your country will not wish to provoke a war for the sake of two very undistinguished naval officers—one of them a deserter!"

"Ah," Halfhyde said, "so you know about that, do you?"

"I have a full report. A shameful business. You have my condolences. The boy should be flogged until there is no flesh left. In Russia he would die, but in your country there are too many woolly-minded old women in places of authority."

"Oh, he'll be dealt with when he's returned to England," Halfhyde said off-handedly. Then his voice hardened. "In the meantime, sir, I must ask this: fair treatment for him, and treatment according to his station. Deserter he may be, but he has yet to face court martial. In my country, whatever the circumstances, a person is officially innocent until proved guilty. So long as *you* insist upon holding us aboard your flagship, *I* must insist that we are treated according to our rank."

Gorsinski, about to give some sharp reply, seemed to change his mind. He looked for a moment at Halfhyde's set face, narrowly, as if weighing something in his mind. Then he swung away, paced the day cabin for some moments, swaying to the roll of the deck, stopping by one of the square ports, looking out over the ornate basketwork of the sternwalk towards the distantly breaking surf. After more thought he swung round on Halfhyde, the morning sun glinting on the gold encrustations of his uniform.

"Very well," he said abruptly. "You shall be treated as you

ask. There are spare cabins—you and the deserter shall occupy one each, under guard. I concede this because I have misgivings as to the wisdom of my seamen and stokers knowing that any officer, even a foreign one, can be treated as a common man. They are but dogs, and must not be given dangerous ideas."

Halfhyde smiled. "You fear them, then?"

"Fear them?" Gorsinski drew himself up, his eyes flashing. "What is this you say? How can I fear them, men of their condition? I have said they are dogs, and dogs they are, and one single act that shows they have ceased to think of themselves as dogs brings down the lash, even the bullet if I say the word!" The Admiral seemed to swell. "I am Prince Gorsinski, second cousin of His Imperial Majesty the Czar of all the Russias himself! I am not to be trifled with, and those dogs know it well."

Halfhyde bowed, hiding a sardonic smile. "As you say, sir, as you say. I am a mere lieutenant without connections and influence, with no royal blood and descended from a simple gunner's mate who fought under Lord Nelson at Trafalgar— bravely as any lord, but the blood he shed was far from blue. Yet I, too, am not to be trifled with, and however humble I may be I am British. So I repeat, sir, by keeping me prisoner you are courting danger for your squadron, for never yet has Great Britain failed her subjects in need—"

"It's a danger I accept readily," the Admiral broke in, sitting down again at his desk. "Now let us talk of other things, Lieutenant Halfhyde." He gestured towards a chair. "You may sit."

"Thank you." Halfhyde sat down and crossed his legs in a comfortable attitude. "What things shall we discuss, sir?"

"First, your presence here. Why have you come?"

Halfhyde said, "You have had a full report—you said as much."

"A report, yes. Now your own words."

"I went overboard after Mr Runcorn."

"A deserter?"

Halfhyde nodded. "Yes."

"You knew, at the time, that he was deserting his ship?"

"No. I believed he had merely fallen in."

"I see." The Admiral looked back at Halfhyde from hooded eyes. "Then he informed you, after the event, that he was in fact deserting? You—his superior officer? Is this so?"

Aware suddenly of danger, Halfhyde paused. Mentally he damned the Board of Admiralty and Captain Fitzsimmons—and himself. Sheer stupidity, sheer dereliction of duty, that all concerned had failed to consider what, in retrospect, was an obvious and important point. Knowing he had to answer fast, he spoke evenly. "Yes, this is quite so, sir. Mr Runcorn was overwrought and frightened when he saw the ship steam away, leaving him many miles from shore. I talked to him kindly, as an older and more experienced officer, and he told me the truth. I think he did not expect to survive, sir."

Prince Gorsinski's stare was direct and bold now. "Then there is no other reason? No hidden reason for your presence on the Slave Coast, Lieutenant Halfhyde?"

"None, sir, none at all."

Gorsinski nodded and smiled. "I am so glad! Had it been otherwise, things might have gone more hardly with you. But I am sure you will forgive me if I make . . . other enquiries in support of your word?"

"You mean, sir?"

Gorsinski smiled again, and took up a heavy round ruler made of ebony, smacking it gently into his palm. "I mean I shall now question your deserter, Lieutenant Halfhyde, that is what I mean!"

When Mr Midshipman Runcorn was brought to the Admiral's cabin, Prince Gorsinski was once more alone. Halfhyde had been taken under escort to a spare cabin as promised, and was currently lying on a bunk with the port open in the ship's side above his head and an armed sentry on guard outside the door, on the inside of which hung blue trousers and a plain white shirt. Mr Runcorn, dressed in similar rig, feeling his bowels desperately loose and a nasty dryness in his mouth stood shaking before the immense majesty of the second cousin of the Czar of all the Russias, only too conscious of the terrible gap between any admiral, even a foreign one, and a midshipman. Prince Gorsinski stood with his back to Mr Runcorn, as though unwilling to so much as look at anything so pernicious as a deserter.

"You deserted your ship, Mr Runcorn."

"Yes, sir." Runcorn, knowing himself not, in fact, to be a deserter at all, answered readily and smartly and without a properly becoming contrition—which angered Prince Gorsinski.

"You sound proud!" he snapped.

"Oh, no, sir!"

"Why did you desert?"

"Sir, I—I . . . there was a lot of bullying, sir."

"You are a coward, Mr Runcorn, a disgrace to your Navy. I spit upon you." Prince Gorsinski, remaining turned away, spat through the square port, his head jerking forward like a striking snake. "You wished, I suppose, the presence of your mother to soften the blows of sea life!"

"Er . . ."

"At sea no man, nor boy either, has a mother. The sea herself is mother to us all, and suckles us well and adequately." Suddenly the Admiral turned, staring now into the midshipman's eyes. He lifted the ebony ruler which was still in his hand, and struck Runcorn heavily across the cheek. The midshipman swung his torso from the blow, but stood his ground. Next the ruler struck from the other side; still Runcorn stood firm, staring back at the Russian admiral, his cheeks wealed and flaming but a light of astonished fury in his eyes. Gorsinski, laughing now, threw the ruler across the cabin. "You are not a coward after all," he said. "You do not cringe from me! Have they not taught you, in the British Navy, to cringe, boy?"

"No, sir."

"A pity. Yet you have told me something. I do not believe you, when you say you deserted from your ship, Mr British Midshipman!"

"But I *did*, sir! Really I did!"

"Then you shall tell me all about it," Gorsinski said, sitting down. "The whole story. Come!"

Runcorn did as he was told, giving his simple story in straight seamanlike fashion.

"On a baulk of timber, you say. And the navigation?"

"The counter-equatorial current, sir."

"Ah yes, the counter-equatorial current, so very convenient for deserters—almost the spot might have been selected, is this not so?"

"It *was* selected, sir. By me. I'm not bad at navigation, sir, and I judged the best place."

"After all the terrible bullying, yes. This 'sub of the gunroom' you told me of, who and what is this?"

The wart explained the lofty functions of Mr Dalrymple-Martin.

"He is very terrible?"

"Very, sir."

"Yet not, I think as terrible as me. You did not hit him, Mr Runcorn?"

"Sir! One doesn't hit a sub-lieutenant, sir!"

Gorsinski nodded. "Yes, this I understand. You preferred to desert, rather than—perhaps in a rage, which I think you are capable of—to hit?"

"Yes, sir."

"I think you were on the point of hitting me."

"Yes, sir. I'm sorry, sir."

"You would not hit a sub-lieutenant—and as I say, I understand this. Yet I am an admiral, and a prince."

"Yes, sir." The midshipman shuffled a little, but still met Gorsinski's eye.

"Some explanation, if you please?"

"Yes, sir. You're a foreigner, sir."

Gorsinski glared. "So! I am a foreigner!" He snapped his fingers. "Very well. I am a *foreigner,* as you say. And you, Mr Runcorn, are not a deserter." Gorsinski's voice hardened as he leaned towards the midshipman, wagging a ringed finger in the latter's face. "Now you will tell me what you really are. You will tell me why you have come here with Lieutenant Halfhyde."

"I *have* told you, sir. I deserted."

Gorsinski stood up, his square, bearded face formidable. "Enough of such nonsense. You will tell me the truth, Mr Runcorn—or I shall take you at your word and assume you are indeed a deserter. In which case I shall act in the room of your own Admiralty and punish you on their behalf."

"I don't understand, sir."

"No? Then allow me to explain, Mr Runcorn. If you do not immediately tell me what I wish to know, I shall send for my Flag Captain. I shall say, 'Captain Borodin, here is a deserter from the British Fleet for punishment. You will prepare for a flogging.'" Gorsinski paused, staring down at the midshipman. "Well, what have you to say, Mr Runcorn?"

"Sir, I have nothing to say."

Gorsinski nodded, and pressed an electric bell-push beside his desk.

Chapter 10

HALFHYDE was brought up, under strong escort, to witness the flogging. Though flogging had long since been abandoned in the Royal Navy, the scene was familiar enough to St Vincent Halfhyde by virtue of his reading of naval history. The *Romanov* was a Russian ship, under steam and not sail, but even so the atmosphere that morning, and the accoutrements of punishment, were similar enough to those long forgotten scenes so frequently enacted aboard British sailing ships-of-war. The ship's company, the men wearing a curiously sullen look, was fallen in along the main deck and at the after end of the midship superstructure; on the starboard side of the quarterdeck, a scrubbed white grating had been triced up to extended stanchions rising from the guardrail, and on that side the awning had been furled to allow a clear view from the superstructure. Between two Russian midshipmen, Mr Runcorn was standing, clad only in his Russian-provided trousers. Ready at the grating stood the ship's master-at-arms, drawing the thin leather thongs of a lead-weighted cat-o'-nine-tails through calloused fingers. The atmosphere—to Halfhyde who would have expected a sense of blood-lust, of anticipation in the inflicting of grotesque pain—was as curious as the sullen expressions of the Russian seamen. It was a brooding, heavy atmosphere in which Halfhyde felt again that unmistakable hostility towards the officers, an atmosphere as pregnantly fermenting as mashed wort in a brewery.

At an order from the *Romanov's* Commander, Runcorn was taken to the grating to be secured by rope lashings around wrists and ankles. Halfhyde, his own face pale with anger, noted the wart's dead-white look, noted also the firm set of the mouth. The boy was going into this with the intention of saying nothing, but Halfhyde knew he could not be blamed if he should break. That tender skin of youth would peel like a banana under the lash.

Halfhyde called out in Russian to Prince Gorsinski, standing to watch from beneath the shade of the quarterdeck awning, "Sir, a word, if you please."

"What is it?"

Halfhyde switched to the English language. "You spoke of officers . . . the men not seeing them poorly treated. Does this performance not give the lie, sir, to your own words?"

"There is a difference, Lieutenant Halfhyde. This is for the special purpose of protecting our imperial interest—for gaining knowledge. The men will understand this. It is not a question of a standard of messing and accommodation."

"Words," Halfhyde said sneeringly, scornfully. "I think you're simply gratifying your own high-class sadism, Prince Gorsinski!"

"You lie, Lieutenant!"

"Then prove your words, sir! Am I not more of an officer than Mr Runcorn?"

"Yes."

"Then, sir, flog me in his place!"

"You?" The Russian laughed. "No, Lieutenant Halfhyde, not you. I think you have a harder skin, and will not talk so easily."

"There is nothing to talk about, sir. You have the facts already."

Gorsinski shook his head. "That is not so. The midshipman has told me that much. He is not a deserter, my friend!" He laughed again.

"Mr Runcorn told you that?"

"Yes, he told me that."

Halfhyde read flat denial in the firm shake of the wart's head. He said loudly, this time in Russian, "You are a liar, Prince Gorsinski, a damned liar, and I spit your lies back in your teeth." Gathering saliva, he spat full in the Russian's face. Spittle drooled down the beard. Gorsinski made an almost animal sound of fury. The men holding Halfhyde twisted his arms up cruelly until he gave an involuntary gasp of pain.

Gorsinski said in a scarcely-controlled voice, "You have your wish, though you have not saved your midshipman, Lieutenant Halfhyde. Now you shall both be flogged—you first, so that the boy can see what he is about to suffer!" He turned away, shaking with anger, giving fresh orders to his Flag Captain. Runcorn was taken down from the grating; Halfhyde, brought across the quarterdeck by his guards, was lashed tight in the midshipman's place. When, shirtless now, he was well secured, the Master-at-Arms made a report to the Commander. In an otherwise total silence, the single beat of a drum was heard from the after end of the midship superstructure. Halfhyde's ordeal commenced. The Master-at-Arms drew back his right arm, sent the cat-o'-nine-tails whistling down across the bared backbone. Halfhyde's body jerked and he bit down hard on the sponge that had been thrust between his teeth. There was a pause, during which Halfhyde was aware of a low growl from the watching seamen, then cries of pain and anger as the ship's police moved in among them with vicious rope's-ends. On the second drumbeat, a petty officer on Halfhyde's right brought down the multi-thonged lash. Thereafter it was an alternate business. Halfhyde lost count after the first dozen or so: there was too much pain, too urgent a need to concentrate his thoughts as wholly as possible on totally different things in an effort to dissociate mind from body. The drumbeats, the dreadful anticipatory pauses, the racking fall of the weighted thongs that wrapped themselves around back and chest and stomach, seemed endless. He was starting to slip into unconsciousness when he heard the raised voice of Prince Gorsinski, dimly, as if from another world: "Stop—stop the punishment, I say."

There was a pause, a long pause, broken by no beat of drum, no agonizing rip of flesh. Halfhyde hung slackly against the bloodstained grating, held by the rope lashings, his mind swimming on a sea of intense pain. Dimly he heard more voices, and the sound of a boat bumping against the lower platform of the accommodation-ladder. Then an order came from the Flag Captain. "Cut down the English officer."

Halfhyde felt himself taken by rough hands as the lashings fell away, lifted from the grating and turned, then set shakily on his own feet. As he staggered, the Russian seamen steadied him, their hands drawing more pain from lacerated flesh. Then he became aware of Prince Gorsinski standing in front of him. Gorsinski said in a soft voice, a dangerous voice, "So your midshipman is a deserter, Lieutenant Halfhyde?"

"Yes."

"You do not wish to change your story?"

"No."

There was a pause, then Gorsinski turned to the Master-at-Arms. "Bring the English officer to my cabin," he said tersely. He turned away towards the hatch. Halfhyde, his legs dragging from time to time so that he had to be virtually carried, was led below, finding the negotiation of the ladder from the hatch an agonizing experience that brought the sweat out all over his body. In the Admiral's quarters he was held by two seamen in front of Prince Gorsinski, whose face held a sadistic smile.

"I ordered a search of Senhora da Luz's premises." Gorsinski said. "I have now the report of the officer in charge. It seems Mr Runcorn was a well-prepared deserter—and you a well-prepared recoverer!" The voice hardened, drumming into Halfhyde's ears. "Two revolvers—not just the one that you drew upon one of my own lieutenants in Fishtown, but two. And a boat's compass, Lieutenant Halfhyde."

"A necessity," Halfhyde said through set teeth, "for any man who goes overboard by intent . . . as you must know."

"I agree, indeed. And perhaps easily enough acquired by a midshipman who wishes to desert from one of Her Majesty's ships . . . but which ship, Lieutenant Halfhyde, which ship?" Through his pain Halfhyde was conscious of rising alarm, but at first did not understand the drift of the Russian's remark. Gorsinski, smiling icily, moved away towards his deck, and came back holding something in his hands. Halfhyde recognized the boat's compass, but still did not understand.

He said as much.

Smiling still, Gorsinski dipped the rose of the compass to one side, and pointed with his forefinger. Halfhyde saw faint marks, and made out numbers scratched into the casing, numbers that were out of sight until the rose was dipped well down.

As understanding came at last, Halfhyde was speechless: the numbers would be a ship's pennant numbers.—He cursed beneath his breath, cursed and damned all over-zealous chief bosun's mates and their tendency to invent their own methods of safeguarding deck gear against dockyard pilfering. Gorsinski, unnecessarily now, filled in the details. "Since I happen to have a copy of your Navy's confidential Fleet Signal Book in my possession, I am able to identify those pennant numbers. They are not those of the *Diadem*, Lieutenant Halfhyde, but those of the *Aurora*."

There was no more brutality; Mr Runcorn was spared his ordeal by lash. Halfhyde was taken from the Admiral's quarters to be attended by the surgeon of the *Romanov,* after which he lay face down on his bunk swathed in bandages covering soothing lotions. Lying there painfully throughout the day, feeling no hunger for the midday meal, he thought furiously. Gorsinski had now exposed the lie. That had to be accepted. But Gorsinski did not know, and would not know from Halfhyde, the present whereabouts of the *Aurora*. He might guess, of course; and in due time he might receive intelligence from incoming vessels. That was something for the future. Halfhyde was more concerned with events recently past. There could have been brutality in Bella da Luz's discreet establishment, and for that he would be immensely regretful. And what of himself and the wart? Why had Prince Gorsinski not continued the floggings in an attempt to discover the *Aurora's* orders from the Admiralty? That must remain a mystery for the time being, but Halfhyde had few doubts that Gorsinski had initially let his temper run away with his discretion and would now be regretting the fact. It was not

just the degrading of an officer, dangerous enough in its impli-
cation that officers were, after all, human flesh and blood.
Halfhyde thought again about the sullen faces of the Russian
seamen, their restiveness. His ordeal that day could yet rebound
upon Prince Gorsinski, could be flung mightily into his sneer-
ing, aristocratic face by a ship's company that could perhaps see
themselves triced up to the grating as Halfhyde had been. It
could prove a crossroads for ill-treated, vengeful men.

Halfhyde's thoughts shifted, moving across the Gulf of Guinea
to the distantly cruising *Aurora,* and to Captain Fitzsimmons.
Halfhyde's mission, in basis a simple one if also dangerous, had
been half completed already. Bella da Luz had seemed to confirm the Russian aims as being to establish trading posts, which
must in the end lead to the creation of an unwelcome sphere
of Russian influence; she had also confirmed the existence of
military fortifications. Halfhyde had yet to see these for himself, and make an assessment of them, and to confirm the
alleged holding of British nationals aboard the *Grand Duke
Alexis.* Had he been at liberty, this would have been easy enough,
but Halfhyde still had reservations as to the possibilities of
effective British action. One ship. . . and no indication from
Fitzsimmons that the admiral in Gibraltar had intended to ask
Whitehall to send more strength, a request that in any event
would take time to reach England.

At three bells in the last dog watch, dinner was brought to
Halfhyde's cabin by a punctiliously polite steward attended by
an armed seaman who stood in the doorway with his rifle while
the meal was served. By now Halfhyde was hungry enough. It
was a fine meal: an excellent clear soup laced with wine, wild
native duckling with a bottle of a good burgundy, avocado pear

and passion fruit. This compared more than favourably with a British wardroom and was much more expertly cooked and served. Halfhyde noted an expression of almost savage resentment on the face of the armed seaman, and hazarded a guess as to the food that would appear in the mess-tins of the ordinary sailors: hard tack and biscuits, preceded on lucky days, perhaps, by pea soup. As in British warships, the actual content and size of the lower deck meals would no doubt depend upon the degree of avarice of the paymaster.

After his meal, Halfhyde, rested now, felt considerably more alive. His wounds were painful still, and would remain so for some days, but they no longer filled his world with their clamourings. When the cabin door was shut and locked, and he was left alone, he knelt on his bunk and looked out of the port towards the shore, a dark tree-backed line lightened along its length by the rushing South Atlantic rollers surging into the Gulf, spray-topped and swift. Distantly he heard their noise, like very far-off thunder as they broke on the sand. Closer at hand there was a slight and rhythmic rattle from the lower platform of the starboard accommodation-ladder, which was almost directly outside his cabin. Already Halfhyde, in spite of his pain, had investigated the possibilities of the port itself, but it was much too small for him to squeeze his body through. He remained kneeling on the bunk for a while, looking out of the port, feeling the wind, the *harmattan,* the dust-laden wind that blew from out of the north-east quadrant, but not, normally, in the wet season after the end of February—the main rains had still not yet come, though they could not now be far off. As to the *harmattan,* Halfhyde devoutly wished it ill. If it should blow strongly enough, the south-easterly set of the current by means of which he would, eventually, rejoin the *Aurora,* could be reversed . . .

At two bells in the first watch Halfhyde was again sent for by Prince Gorsinski. He found the Admiral, in full mess dress and smoking a cigar, sitting in an armchair outside on his stern walk. Gorsinski rose when the British officer was brought in, coming in himself from the stern-walk and closing the access door behind him. Gorsinski pointed with his cigar to a chair.

"Sit down, my friend. You'll join me in a glass of armagnac?"

Halfhyde shrugged, and sat with his body well clear of the chair's back. "Why not? Though I happen to prefer cognac."

"Then cognac you shall have." Gorsinski gestured peremptorily to his petty officer servant, who crossed the day cabin with a decanter and a glass. Cognac was poured; Gorsinski sent the servant away, and raised his glass. "To His Imperial Majesty the Czar of all the Russias."

Halfhyde also raised his glass, and politely drank the toast. Gorsinski then raised his again. "To Her Majesty the Queen Empress, Queen Victoria."

"She also is imperial, sir."

"Your pardon." Gorsinski repeated the toast, this time correctly, and the two officers drank. Gorsinski perambulated the cabin for a while, frowning, pulling at his cigar, hands clasped behind his back. Then he stopped, and asked, "You are still in pain, Lieutenant Halfhyde?"

"Damnably so, but no matter. I'm no child, and I shall heal soon. It's you who should be concerned, Prince Gorsinski."

"Ah? How so?"

Halfhyde shrugged. "Her Imperial Majesty, Queen Victoria, has long arms for a small woman. And for a small country we have much strength." Halfhyde set his glass down with a bang on a walnut table by his chair. "My hurts will be avenged as soon as word reaches London."

"Which it will not do."

Halfhyde looked up, a faint smile on his lips. "You think not, sir? You really think not? You don't think your men will talk ashore—that word of this morning's damnable act will not already have reached Fishtown? If you think that, then you don't know the natives as well as I do, I assure you! And the moment a British ship enters, she'll get the word and then carry it back to London and the British Admiralty." Halfhyde laughed. "Wars have been declared for less and I doubt if the court at St Petersburg has any wish to take on the British Empire."

Gorsinski gave a careless gesture. "Times are changing fast. Great countries no longer go to war for the hacking off of a nautical ear. And St Petersburg is concerned with more important things than to reprimand me for flogging a man . . . who happens to be wanted in Sevastopol for murder."

Halfhyde stared, rising a little in his chair. "Murder? There was no murder! None, d'you hear me? My escape—"

"Was carried out cunningly and bloodlessly—oh, yes, I know that, Lieutenant Halfhyde!"

"Then—"

"Nevertheless, a man in fact died that night—a drunk, who fell into the harbour and drowned, after striking his head on the jetty. A seaman of the Black Sea Fleet." Gorsinski paused, pulling at his beard, then went on in a heavy, deliberate tone, "This morning, before the flogging, I conducted my own investigation into the events of that night—"

"You damned liar!"

"Questioning—for the first time—that seaman's death." The Russian aristocrat pointed a finger at Halfhyde. "You admitted your responsibility, Lieutenant Halfhyde."

"I?"

"Silence, my friend Halfhyde!" Gorsinski loomed over him threateningly. "And have a care. My sentry will come in at the first sound of trouble, and he will shoot. A self-confessed murderer deserves no trial and no second chance. And I . . . I am Prince Gorsinski, allied to the blood royal of Russia. I shall not be disbelieved in St Petersburg, and I shall have my revenge on a man who threw my favours back in my teeth by escaping! God has been kind in delivering you to me, Lieutenant Halfhyde."

"God," Halfhyde said tartly, "may yet have second thoughts. Or do you propose, having already mounted a flogging, to mount an immediate execution as well?"

Gorsinski shook his head. "I do not. I think you have things to tell, and you shall tell them." He sat down again, facing Halfhyde, large square hands laid upon his knees. "Come, my dear fellow, you have nothing to lose now, and much to gain. Think about this. Whatever happens, you are going back with me to Russia in due course. But you are still master of your own fate, of your future inside Russia."

Chapter 11

IT was a case of blow hot, blow cold; but whatever the promises that alternated with the threats, Gorsinski was Halfhyde's implacable enemy and Halfhyde had no intention of allowing himself to forget it. As to his orders, the Admiral had without much difficulty arrived at a deduction: Britain had an interest in the Russian trading aspirations. He put this to his prisoner.

Halfhyde shrugged. "I dare say that's true, but it's no concern of mine."

"No?" Gorsinski regarded him musingly, broodingly. "Once we had an understanding, you and I. I thought much of you . . . and was of service, if you care to remember, securing your release from Siberia.

"I was grateful, sir."

"You would like to return there."

"I would not. It's a hell on earth, if one can use the word hell in connection with such fiendish cold." Remembrance alone of his terrible days and nights in the bitter Siberian wind made Halfhyde shiver. "But you'll not expect me to avoid it by any traitorous act. As a naval officer yourself, you'd not really expect that, Prince Gorsinski."

"Brave words, my friend!"

Halfhyde smiled. "Prudent ones, rather than brave. It's my

intention to rejoin the British Fleet at the first possible moment, and I've no wish to rejoin it in disgrace."

"You are foolishly over-confident, Lieutenant Halfhyde. Let us return to the business of trading. Trading is a peaceful business, is it not? We Russians have a right to trade, as you have. Why is the British Admiralty concerned in this?"

Again Halfhyde shrugged. "I didn't say it was. But let's assume, since you seem to wish it, that it is. What about the question of our own sea links with South Africa, with Cape Town and Simon's Town?"

"There would be no interference," Gorsinski said shortly.

"It might come, in time."

"In time, anything might come! The world does not stand still. But if your country is concerned about our trading posts, Lieutenant Halfhyde, what then does she propose to do about them? Are you perhaps here to survey the coast, with the intention of preparing maps for the landing of a British force? Is this your mission?"

Halfhyde yawned insolently in Gorsinski's face. "Not so far as I know. It would be unnecessary in any case, since I already have a special knowledge of the Bight of Benin. After leaving Sevastopol, I served here on the coast, and grew to know these seas well, as a navigator. Had the Admiralty desired to pick my brains, they would have kept me in London rather than send me here. And about trade I know nothing and care less. Trade is not for seamen, Prince Gorsinski."

"But your government—"

"I have not the foggiest notion what lies in the mind of my government," Halfhyde broke in, reflecting, with an inward smile, that this statement was most certainly true. Gorsinski leapt suddenly to his feet, his fists bunched, his patience seeming to give way. Halfhyde was about to rise from his own seat, bracing himself against possible physical attack, when there was the sound of a raised voice outside the day cabin and, without knocking, the Flag Captain Borodin, came in looking grimly angry.

The Admiral stared. "Captain Borodin, what—"

"Your pardon, Your Highness." Borodin glanced down at Halfhyde, then back at Gorsinski. "There is trouble on the stokers' mess deck, Your Highness."

"Trouble? What trouble, Borodin?"

"Refusal of an order, Your Highness. A party of stokers who were holding a meeting . . . they refuse to disperse on the orders of the Master-at-Arms."

"Then send an officer, Borodin!"

"Your Highness, that has been done. The Commander went, and his order was also refused."

Gorsinski stared. "This is mutiny!"

"Not yet, Your Highness. It has not spread beyond the one group of men, and—"

"Then we shall ensure that it does *not* spread, Flag Captain!" Gorsinski crossed the cabin with long strides, and opened a locked steel cupboard. He brought out a revolver and spun the chambers, then loaded, his eyes blazing with anger. "Where is the Commander now, Borodin?"

"Your Highness, he is with the Master-at-Arms at the scene of the—"

"In danger, do you think?"

Borodin nodded. "Possibly, Your Highness—"

"You will have the lower deck cleared, Flag Captain, if you please, at once. The ship's company to muster on the fo'c'sle, all officers to arm themselves and report to the quarterdeck, petty officers to muster on the upper deck on either side of the midship superstructure so as to place themselves between the officers and the men. At once, Borodin!"

"Your Highness." The Flag Captain turned about and hurried from the Admiral's quarters.

Gorsinski pointed his revolver at Halfhyde and ordered him on his feet. Halfhyde was pushed to the outer door, to be taken over by his armed escort. Gorsinski ordered the prisoner to be marched back to his cabin. Halfhyde, trying to read the man's face before he was pushed ahead of the bayonet, found inscrutability: the fellow could come down on either side, depending which way events should move in the next few minutes. There was the usual quiet in the after section of the ship, at least until the sound of a bugle came stridently, shattering the calm. When that happened, officers came out of the wardroom and from cabins, making for the rack where arms were stowed as the Flag Captain's voice was heard passing the order. There was a rush for the ladder up to the quarterdeck as Halfhyde was once again locked in his cabin. After this came more bugle calls, the sound of footsteps milling about overhead, then a curious and foreboding silence. Halfhyde, feeling excitement and tension mount in him, waited, gnawing at his fingernails. For a while nothing seemed to happen. The silence continued. Halfhyde found it almost unbearable: to be caught up in a Russian mutiny was the last thing he wanted. To men treated for so long as dogs, an officer might be an officer, and never mind his nationality. There was beginning to be a kind of international aspect to the reaction of common men to the topweight of autocracy, a reaction that had not passed unnoticed even in England. To die spitted like a pig on the bayonet of a maddened Russian sailor as a mob swept through the flagship would be bitter indeed!

Halfhyde moved in the small cabin, two paces one way, two paces back, a caged animal himself with no love for Russian princes. He sweated, as much from his anxiety and frustration as from the humid heat of the Bight of Benin. In a tricky situation such as incipient mutiny, he placed little reliance in the methods of Russian aristocrats; and one wrong step now could precipitate a bloodbath. The silence continued still, bringing with it its own increasing fear. Halfhyde mistrusted that silence with a deep inner certainty that it boded very ill indeed.

When it ended, and ended abruptly, he was far from surprised at the manner of its breaking.

Distantly, he heard a single revolver shot. At first that was all; after it, the silence seemed even more intense yet at the same time more fragile; and it ended again in a sound like baying—a rising roar of men's voices, hoarse and defiant and with more than a trace of a wild exultancy and triumph. Halfhyde hammered on his door, shouting for the sentry outside to open up. There was no response. Again from the distance there were shots, this time many of them, a fusillade from rifles and revolvers, followed by a rush of feet overhead, some of them booted, others bare, a flowing and menacing wave of sound. Then came a long-drawn cry, a high scream of agony and death. From outside Halfhyde's cabin port came the sound of a splash. Scrambling up on the bunk, he looked out. A gold-laced body, a body in mess dress, floated by the end of the accommodation-ladder, face downwards, arms outstretched. As Halfhyde watched, another body fell from the quarterdeck— Flag Captain Borodin.

Halfhyde took a deep breath. The course was now clear enough! Full-scale mutiny, and all that went with it. One shot had been indiscreetly fired, and the rest followed as the night the day.

Above now, the ship was in total uproar: shouts, shots, cries and oaths. The *Romanov* had swung to the tide, and Halfhyde's cabin was now looking to seaward. He saw boats coming off from the other two ships of the squadron, and it was anybody's guess as to whether they brought help for the Flag or more mutineers: mutiny had an uncomfortable way of spreading once established, and the men of the *St Petersburg* and the *Grand Duke Alexis* might well have decided to take their chance at a propitious moment. Once more Halfhyde hammered on his door. Currently he was something of a rat in a trap, and that was an unpleasant feeling. There was no response; and listening with his ear close to the door he could hear no evidence of the sentry. He tested the door with his shoulder: it was secure, strong. But not for long. As Halfhyde stood pondering, casting round for some means of attacking the door, a rush of footsteps came into the flat outside and men were heard shouting and crying out. There was rifle fire, more cries, then a splintering of woodwork as a heavy rifle-butt smashed into a panel of Halfhyde's cabin door. He stood back and away, expecting bullets: none came. The fighting moved on, died away out of earshot, but there was still a battle raging on the deck above. Halfhyde tore at the splintered wood, clearing the panel. Looking out, he saw that the sentry had deserted his post. He took up the discarded suit of white duck, still hanging over the back of a chair, tore off his shirt and trousers, pulled on the anonymous duck uniform, and heaved himself through the gaping panel into the flat outside. There was a sharp smell of burnt gunpowder. His face tight, Halfhyde made for Runcorn's cabin: as he did so a heavy body tumbled down the ladder from the quarterdeck, the body of a bearded able seaman still holding his rifle and bayonet. Halfhyde pried the butt from clenched fingers, took the ammunition-belt from the body, strapped it round his own, then ran for the wart's cabin. He thumped on the door, hard.

"You there—Wart! It's me, Halfhyde—"

"Sir!"

"Stand clear of the lock, Wart, for your life."

"Aye, aye, sir."

Halfhyde unfixed the bayonet and put the muzzle of the rifle against the door-lock. He fired: the lock came away enough for the rifle-butt to do the rest. From round the angle of the door came Mr Runcorn, saluting. "Never mind that!" Halfhyde snapped. "We cut and run while we have the chance. On deck with you—at the double!" He ran for the quarterdeck ladder, bare feet thudding on the steel deck. With Runcorn close behind, he went up fast and emerged behind his rifle, with bayonet fixed again, into a shambles, a seething mass of fighting officers and men. A lieutenant lunged at him with a cutlass, which he dodged. Another Russian officer came in behind; just in time, Halfhyde swung round and saw the revolver's muzzle within inches of the wart's skull. He seized the wrist, twisted it viciously, and the bullet discharged full into the throat of a coal-blackened stoker, who fell to the deck clutching at his shattered windpipe and making animal-like noises. Then Halfhyde saw the Admiral himself, fighting back bravely in company with his Flag Lieutenant and another officer. Prince Gorsinski, his face grim but his gaze steady, held a cutlass in his right hand, a revolver in the left. He was fighting to good effect, apparently untouched himself, and was clearly acting as a rallying-point for his officers and such men as had remained loyal. As their eyes met, Halfhyde saw recognition in Gorsinski's face. The admiral snapped an order and two officers detached from his small fighting group and cut their way through towards Halfhyde and the midshipman. Halfhyde felt the thrust of cold steel in his ribs as a thick arm went around his throat.

"Resist and you are dead," a voice said in his ear. The arm tightened, and the steel pressed harder. Halfhyde felt himself pushed willy-nilly through the fighting mob, urged towards the after hatch to the Admiral's quarters. In the stench of gunsmoke and spilt blood, and the pungent sweat of desperately fighting sailors, he was pushed along till he reached the hatchway. Then he was lifted off his feet and flung clear down to the deck below. In falling he managed to get a grip on the steel ladder, from which, bruised and winded, he hung; a moment later Runcorn came down, head over heels and yelling with alarm, to send Halfhyde crashing to the deck. Behind came the Russian officers, and behind them again, Prince Gorsinski and the Flag Lieutenant, the latter with blood pouring from a scalp wound. Halfhyde and Runcorn were ordered to their feet and propelled towards the Admiral's cabin. Outside, as they came in sight, the sentry crashed to attention. Halfhyde heard Gorsinski say, as he came up to the man, "Loyal fellow! You shall be rewarded, never fear!"

They entered the cabin; here all was peace, the sounds of fighting muted. Halfhyde and Runcorn were ordered to stand with their backs to a bulkhead under guard of a junior officer, who first searched them for arms. Gorsinski, breaking off from a muttered word with his Flag Lieutenant, strode across.

"My apologies, Lieutenant Halfhyde. I much regret this situation, but it will be contained, you may be sure—"

Halfhyde cut in with a laugh. "Don't be too confident, Your Highness!" He gestured towards the fore part of the ship. "There's power there, the power of numbers. They've gone too far to give way. D'you suppose they'll stop fighting now, and surrender to hang from your yard-arms, Prince Gorsinski?"

Gorsinski's face was grey but formidable. He said, "There are loyal men amongst them—"

"Loyal men, or loyal dogs?"

"As you wish, Lieutenant Halfhyde, the term is not important now."

"It has been, Prince Gorsinski, it has been! You've turned your ship into a powder-barrel by contemptuous treatment of good men. In the British Navy we treat men as men, not as dogs."

"Silence!" His face livid, the Admiral shook a fist at Halfhyde. "You are in danger as well as I, and you will do well to be constructive now. Will you act as an officer, and help me to control my flagship? Or do you wish to identify yourself with the seamen and stokers?"

Again Halfhyde smiled. "I haven't the chance," he observed, "to do the latter, Prince Gorsinski. But I'm damned if I'm going to help *you*. It's no skin off my nose."

"Then you will remain under guard, you and your midshipman."

"If I agreed to help, would we be released? Is that what you're offering?"

Gorsinski nodded. "Yes, but subject to your parole, your word that you would not—" He broke off, swinging round towards the door as a thunderous knocking came. He strode across, almost into the arms of a breathless petty officer and a rush of words.

Gorsinski lifted a hand. "Calm yourself, man! More slowly if you wish to be heard."

"Your Highness," the petty officer said, his eyes staring. The ship . . . we are on fire forward . . . burning badly, and—"

"Where are the fire parties, man?" Gorsinski's beard was thrust forward, and his eyes were almost luminous with fury. "Where is my Flag Captain, where is the Commander?"

"Captain Borodin is dead, Your Highness. The Commander was last seen by the after funnel. Your Highness, the men refuse to fight the fires. There are no fire parties left to use."

Prince Gorsinski's face suffused and his body seemed to swell. "I shall take charge personally," he said. He glared round at his remaining officers. "Come—you, sir," he added to the young officer guarding Halfhyde and Runcorn, "you will remain and be responsible that the prisoners do not get away."

"Yes, Your Highness."

Gorsinski left the cabin with his small retinue. Halfhyde glancing sideways at Runcorn, gave him a wink of encouragement; smiling at the guarding officer, he said in Russian, "The ship is in danger, my friend, is it not?"

"I do not think so. The Admiral will mend matters."

"By his personal example?"

"Yes."

"And his fearful presence?"

The officer's eyes narrowed. "I do not understand."

"No? Nor, I think, will the men, who will have lost their fear of princes by now, seeing only the over-riding necessity to make their mutiny a complete success. Prince Gorsinski will get nowhere, my friend. The *Romanov* is doomed. And now I'll tell you something else: if you wish to die on one of your country's bayonets, I do not. If you believe—" Halfhyde broke off suddenly, fixing a stare on the stern-walk behind the officer's back. *"Look out!"*

The young Russian turned. In a flash, Halfhyde flung himself bodily on him and brought him to the deck with a crash, laughing at the easy success of an old trick. Runcorn, reacting fast, bent and grabbed for the officer's revolver, twisting it away from the fingers. The man fought like a wildcat, but was no match for Halfhyde's sinewy strength. Rolling the man over, Halfhyde sat on his chest, gripped his ears, and banged the back of his head hard on the cabin deck, then picked him up bodily, holding the forearms close in to the sides, and hurled him with considerable force at a steel bulkhead. The officer dropped, limp and slack, to the deck, and Halfhyde dusted his hands with a look of satisfaction in his eyes.

"Stern-walk!" he snapped at the wart. "And hang onto that revolver." He led the way out to the stern-walk and hauled his body through the protective basket-work, hanging on outboard of the ship's hull. After him went Runcorn, squeezing through rather more easily, the revolver thrust into his waistband. Halfhyde said, "All right, away you go!"

"Where to, sir?"

"For God's sake, boy, where the devil d'you think?"

"The *Aurora*, sir?"

Halfhyde snapped, "Not unless you can swim twenty-five miles or so, which *I* can't! The shore, Mr Runcorn, the shore! Keep with me."

"Aye, aye, sir."

Halfhyde, pushing out from the stern-walk, dropped into the sea with a splash, the salt water stinging his wealed body cruelly. Going deep for a while, he came up to an astonishing and awesome sight. As dead bodies drifted past him on the heavy swell with white staring faces and outstreched, half-submerged limbs in what looked like a sea of blood, a hugely spreading glow came from the fore part of the *Romanov,* a glow that reddened the night-dark waters of the Bight, a glow that was spreading with remarkable speed and ferocity. From the sides of the ship men were diving into the bloody scum that covered the sea, their swimming heads dotting the way towards the breakers. Looking up as he heard a voice that carried clear above the sounds of the fires and the fighting that was still going on, Halfhyde saw the cruiser's commander standing dangerously on the after end of the superstructure. The commander, outlined by the fires, was shouting through a megaphone to the boats from the two ships in company, telling the crews to lay alongside and board to fight the fires. There was complete confusion, complete chaos; the ship was utterly out of the control of her remaining officers, and the fires raged unchecked, presumably, Halfhyde reckoned, to sweep right through the ship below decks unimpeded by the closing of the watertight doors that might have acted as preventers.

Treading water, conscious of the filthy stench of the scum, Halfhyde looked around for Runcorn; seeing him in the glow, he swam towards him.

"Mr Runcorn!"

The wart turned in relief. "Sir?"

"Get moving, Mr Runcorn. Keep out of the way of the others. If we're parted, we meet at Senhora da Luz's place."

"But Prince Gorsinski, sir—"

Halfhyde laughed. "His Highness will have other matters to attend to now, if he survives at all. We'll chance that. So swim, Mr Runcorn, swim for your life!"

"Aye, aye, sir."

"We're going to come through, never fear—but I doubt if the *Romanov*'s going to wear the Admiral's flag much longer!"

Runcorn, spluttering and gasping, asked, "How's that, sir?"

"The fires," Halfhyde answered. "She's glowing red-hot through her plates already. If I was asked for my opinion, I'd say the magazines'll blow." The midshipman rolled over, looking up towards the foundering flagship. On the fo'c'sle the roaring flames were licking greedily up around the fringes of a great hole in the deck; and in the outboard darkness around the ship's side the glow could be seen clearly as the flames within the hull did their work of destruction, and trails of steam rose from the waterline.

Runcorn rolled over again, and, with Halfhyde keeping by his side, struck out through the scummy surface muck, the rotted outpourings of the Benin and Escravos rivers. The ground swell, setting strongly towards the shore, carried them fast into the outer line of surf. They roared through it, gasping, flung like lifeless corks, battered by spray and solid water. Past Halfhyde, as he came through and stormed on for the next trial of strength and endurance, came a ship's boat filled with sailors, men who stared fearfully and gripped the gunwhales for their lives as the boat, strongly built but a fragile thing in the surf, rushed like the very wind. It vanished over the next breaking crest ahead; and when he had fought his own way through behind, Halfhyde saw the boat once again—upside down and drifting forlornly, its human freight scattered and gone. Pounded—as it felt—to a pulp, Halfhyde was flung willy-nilly through the last line of surf, the real beach-breaker, coming through dropping tons of water to be smashed down on the sand. It had been a worse experience than the original inward crossing of the bar. He lay gasping, semi-conscious, gripped by the sucking drag of the undertow that threatened to pull him back towards the Russian flagship. Just in time, he was seized by a huge Russian sailor and dragged clear, to be dumped unceremoniously on the beach some way farther up.

For a while he lay motionless, gathering such strength as he could. When he lifted his head, roused himself, and stood up, there was no sign of Runcorn. As he moved on, searching among the living and the dead, for the beach was littered with the flung bodies of men who had lost the battle of the breakers, the whole sky lit suddenly: a tremendous, vivid flash from seaward that showed up the trees behind the little township, and the crowds of Jekris staring in awe along the upper part of the beach. As more of the sailors poured in along the line of pounding surf, the huge explosion aboard the *Romanov* shook the land and sea, a thousand thunderstorms breaking violently into the night. It was a terrible sight; in the brilliant light Halfhyde's face was ashen and disturbed. One moment the ship appeared intact, the next she had split, her whole forward section dropping away, her back broken, and the bows pitching down into the water. There was a roar of steam following the first explosion; hard upon its heels came the second great shockwave as the after magazines went up. From the beach men watched transfixed, seemingly unable to leave the vicinity until the dying flagship had gone finally. Then, as the after part, following the bows, shattered away and dropped, and the brilliance of the light began to die, there came a rising murmur from the crowds of Russian seamen, a murmur that grew to a fearsome baying roar. Then, as fists were shaken in the air, a great cheer broke out, rising time and again from the many throats, a frightening cheer of victory, of hate, of revenge.

Halfhyde was still staring out across the water, visualizing the broken remains of power that would be settling in some three and a half fathoms of water, when a delighted hail of relief reached him. The wart, visible in the light of flaming native torches, was running up to him with almost a dog's welcome.

Halfhyde no more than glanced at him. Runcorn, in some surprise, found himself bidden to shut his mouth, and saw Halfhyde's lips moving silently thereafter. A few moments later Halfhyde spoke again, sadly. "My apologies, Wart. I was praying."

"*Praying*, sir?"

"I prayed that God might have mercy on the men that have died out there tonight." He waved a hand out over the water. "No seaman likes to see a ship go down, Wart, and you'll discover that for yourself one day, no doubt. Nor do I personally like the filthy smell of mutiny."

"It's worked on our side tonight, sir . . . so far, anyway."

Halfhyde nodded. "Aye, it has. And I still don't like it, Mr Runcorn! However, I'm glad at least to find you safe and sound."

"Yes, sir. Thank you, sir."

"And now let us get away to hell and out of it, before mutiny turns on us as well! We're going to see some fireworks when the rest of the squadron puts landing parties ashore!"

They turned away. As they did so, the final roar came from the *Romanov*, whose funnel-tops had now evidently dipped below the water. A blast of steam came out as the boiler-rooms were deluged, and a long low rumble came across the water; then silence. Halfhyde and Runcorn moved on up the shelving beach, and Halfhyde held out a hand before his face.

"Rain," he said. "The first since we've been here. Perhaps this is the real start, or perhaps it's just the false one yet—but we shall see, and if it is the start, then we'll be lucky to have a dry stitch of clothing from now on, Wart."

Hard on the heels of those first few drops, as though the tremendous explosion upon the sea had shaken the very heavens into their belated activity, the downpour started, accompanied by a rising wind. Runcorn had never imagined rain on such a scale. In seconds the high part of the beach was covered with water rushing down to the sea. The rain sliced down in almost solid sheets, blotting out the sea and land. When they reached the harder surface behind the beach itself, the rain bounced up around their knees to form a density of spray that gave the feeling that they were walking through floodwater.

Behind them, heading for the cover of jungle country, came the survivors of the mutineers. Halfhyde, shouting in the wart's ear that this indeed was the real start of the rains, found his eye caught by more movement out to sea, beyond the surf. Through the pounding rain-curtain he made out the lights of boats, presumably from the *Grand Duke Alexis* and the *St Petersburg,* heading inshore, to make the crossing of the sand-bar towards the jetty inside the Benin river.

Chapter 12

AS Halfhyde banged loudly on the door of Senhora da Luz's establishment, a thunderstorm broke, right overhead by the sound of it. It was a reverberating crack that shook the very earth and rattled the rotten timbers of Fishtown almost as badly as the exploding *Romanov*. Cursing viciously, the sodden lieutenant banged again.

The door opened, a mere crack. "Who is it?" a voice asked.

"Two drowned rats. Come on, open up, for God's sake!" Halfhyde gave the door an unceremonious push, and went in with Runcorn behind him. The doorkeeper was the native who had admitted them on their first visit, Halfhyde snapped at the man to take them to Senhora da Luz at once. It turned out that the senhora was not at home.

"Where, then?"

"Bwana, madame was taken by canoe to one of the ships."

"*Taken?*"

"On business, bwana."

"Ah—I see! Business. Not revenge?"

"Bwana?"

"I refer," Halfhyde said impatiently, "to her involvement with myself and my midshipman. When I was taken by the Russians, I heard cries on leaving. You will tell me what happened."

"Yes, bwana. There was questioning, and canes were used, but not on the senhora, only on the girls. The captains of the ships protect the senhora, bwana. Her absence today is business, trade, nothing else."

Halfhyde nodded. "I see. Which ship has she gone to?"

"The *St Petersburg,* bwana. For the captain."

With a grin Halfhyde said, "I'll bet she'll be back directly, as things have turned out! We'll not stay though. I don't want to embarrass the senhora, who'll be suffering an influx of the Russian Navy once the squadron's boats come alongside the jetty—those of them, that is, that are not broken on the bar!" He added, "As for you . . . you've not seen us tonight, mind!"

"No, bwana."

"If you open your mouth," Halfhyde said threateningly, "the senhora, and this I guarantee, will have your hide off you with a carving knife!"

"Yes, bwana. I say nothing." The eyes rolled.

"Good," Halfhyde said. "Now I have business in the senhora's sitting-room, then we'll be off."

"Bwana—"

"Out of my way," Halfhyde snapped. He thrust the man aside, and marched with Runcorn to the sitting-room. Inside, he went straight to a corner of the room and pulled up a section of carpet, rolling it back from the wall to a point half-way across the room. "Weapons," he said to Runcorn, "to back up your Russky revolver. I have firsthand knowledge of the senhora's self-preservative instincts!" On hands and knees, he lifted a loose floorboard and reached down, going in to the shoulder, an expression of concentration on his lean face. "Ah—there we are now!" He brought out two small pistols with ivory handles, together with boxes of cartridges. "Ladylike—but they kill at the sort of range the senhora is accustomed to!" He reached in again; out came an assortment of knives and daggers. Halfhyde selected two short-handled pieces with long wavy-edged blades. "Nasty," he said as he re-stowed the remainder.

"Yes, sir."

Halfhyde looked up sardonically. "Not British, Wart?"

"Very much *not,* sir!" The voice was stiff.

"Oh, you'll get used to it," Halfhyde said with a chuckle. "We British happen to be in a minority in this imperfect world, and there are times when we have to make shift with things we'd rather not. It's amazing what a difference the threat of death can make, and chivalry, while wholly admirable, of course, can be suicide when you're dealing, as we shall deal, with mutineers facing death themselves." He put the floorboard back neatly, then spread out the carpet again and stood up. "Now we're ready."

"To do what, sir?"

"To go back into the damned wind and rain, Wart, but not, I hope, for too long. You'll see." Halfhyde made for the door, where the black servant was waiting obsequiously. Halfhyde nodded at him, said, "Your mouth as tight shut as Old Mossy Face, remember," and strode on down the hall. Once they were outside in the torrential rain, Runcorn had an enquiry to make.

"Sir, who is Old Mossy Face?"

Halfhyde gave a shout of laughter. "Oh, to be sweetly innocent again! Old Mossy Face, Mr Runcorn, is an old-fashioned name for the female organ . . . our black friend won't have understood, no doubt, but he'll have got the gist. As a matter of fact . . ."

"Yes, sir?"

"I rather hope he hasn't heard the reference before, since the nature of his employer's business would lead him to associate openness, rather than closure, with the organ referred to."

Invisible in the darkness, Mr Runcorn's face flamed in embarrassment.

There was carnage that night as Prince Gorsinski's avenging boats swept in across the bar for the Benin river. That bar was very hard sand, and was liable to shift, and to break heavily right across; three boats with their full crews and armed parties were lost, and all hands drowned. Some men were lost from the other boats, the ones that managed to reach the jetty, also. But plenty survived the ordeal, and indeed, as the boats discharged armed patrols, it was the blinding rain that was Halfhyde's and Runcorn's temporary salvation. Each patrol, alert and well supplied with rifles and bayonets, was commanded by two officers with express orders to shoot any of their own seamen should they appear likely to show sympathy with the *Romanov's* mutineers.

In one of the boats that made the jetty in safety was the Admiral himself, who, having at last prudently jumped overboard from his foundering ship, had been picked up from the sea by a cutter from the *St Petersburg,* to which ship he had, if only notionally thus far, transferred his flag. Gorsinski's personal order, passed to all hands, was that the mutinous dogs were to be given no opportunity of surrender but were to be shot down on sight. If the loyal should suffer with the disloyal, then this must lead only to a greater degree of obedience on the part of the crews of the *St Petersburg* and her consort, and a greater degree of vigilance against mutiny on the part of those in authority. So the armed parties, pouring from the boats into the tropical downpour, fanned out to begin the round-up as best they could in current conditions.

Halfhyde, moving at the double now, in and out of the dirty, muddy tracks between the shanties of Fishtown, heard sounds of shooting from time to time, coming from many different sectors. He could see nothing himself, and from time to time both he and Runcorn had been blown by the gusting gale into the flimsy sides of the shacks, and had fallen messily into the mud. The avenging Russians, he fancied, were firing blind or at shadows, simply trying to scare the mutineers, or else being trigger-happy in their desperate anxiety to placate their officers. At one point Halfhyde dragged Runcorn out of sight only just in time, as instinct told him of men coming up behind. Scarcely breathing, they hid in the lee of a great bank of stacked earth, now liquifying into mud, as the search party went past behind rifles with fixed bayonets.

"What's going to happen at dawn, sir?" Runcorn asked when the Russians had gone on.

"We won't be on the streets by then, Wart!"

Runcorn asked no further questions: Halfhyde was a poor giver of information. Runcorn, weary and cold now, and also frightened to death though he would never have confessed it, shook with thankfulness when Halfhyde, giving an exclamation of pleasure, at last stopped by what seemed to be a trader's store, a single storey building with a verandah and wide, shuttered windows. There was a lamp burning behind the shutters. Halfhyde hammered on the door, shielded a little now from the rain by the deep roof of the verandah. From outside, at the rear of the premises, guinea-fowl set up a raucous screech. Inside, the lamp flickered, moving to the door, which, like that of Senhora da Luz, opened a mere crack.

"Who's there?"

"An old friend, Mr MacDougall."

"Well now, I'll be buggered! That voice I know." The door came open. An old man, white-haired, red-faced, stood looking. Halfhyde went in, reaching out his hand, and smiling widely. The old trader gasped with surprise and pleasure. "Mr Halfhyde himself! Goodness gracious me! Were ye blown from yon prison ship, or what?"

"You saw it, then?"

"Jesus, I couldna help seeing! It near blew ma bloody roof off!"

"Shut the door, then, Mr MacDougall, or you'll get blown back to Glasgow yourself. The wind's devilish strong." Halfhyde threw water from face and hair and eyes. "God, but it's a filthy night—and there's been some filthy work too, and more to come." He reached out to MacDougall, laying a hand on his shoulder and looking into deep-set eyes, straight eyes beneath craggy white brows. "You'll give us shelter and a bed, for old times' sake?"

MacDougall nodded. "I'll do that, and with pleasure. Come along now, and tell me what's been happening, both tonight and over the years since you were last on the coast, Mr Halfhyde."

They followed the Scotsman into a comfortable living room, where MacDougall set the lamp on a table covered with a green baize cloth. "You can both do with some breakfast, I'm thinking," he said, with a wink at Halfhyde as he brought a bottle of whisky from a cupboard. He poured three generous drams, setting the glasses of neat spirit before the shivering pair. "Get that down your throats, and the clothes off your backs, gentlemen. I have some gear for you to wear while that lot's drying out."

"Thank you," Halfhyde said. He downed the whisky, feeling it glow gratefully. Runcorn took his slowly, sipping it while he stripped off his sodden clothing. The wind plucked at the building, shaking the wooden walls. MacDougall took the wet garments away, returning with clean shirts and trousers; the fit was curious, for MacDougall was short and square, but they cared nothing for that. MacDougall poured more whisky.

"There are beds when you want them," he said, "but if you wish for talk, then I'm listening."

Halfhyde nodded. "There's a lot to tell you, and a lot to ask you too. You'll forgive me if I don't satisfy your own curiosity on all points, though, Mr MacDougall. There's a certain amount of secrecy in this business."

"Aye," MacDougall said, "and I can guess what's behind it without much difficulty." He waved a hand in the direction of the sea. "Yon bloody Russky warships are here for no good purpose—no good purpose from our viewpoint, that is!"

"You mean the traders?"

"Aye, the traders." MacDougall paused. "And the Empire too."

Halfhyde asked, "Why do you say that?"

Macdougall shrugged and took a mouthful of whisky. "I have my reasons, Mr Halfhyde. First, perhaps you'll tell me a little of your part in what's going on?"

"All right," Halfhyde said. "We're old friends, Mr MacDougall, and I trust you never to repeat any of this to a third party."

"Aye, that's understood."

Concisely, Halfhyde explained what had led to his current problem and gave the Scot a summary of past events, including his earlier captivity in Russia and his association with Prince Gorsinski in those days. "When I was given my present orders," he said, "it was not known that Prince Gorsinski himself would be here in the Bight. That was bad luck."

"Aye, it was. And made no better by your attack on the Russian lieutenant," MacDougall said with a grin. "The passing years have not moderated your temper, Mr Halfhyde! But now, how can I be of service?"

Halfhyde leaned across the table. "Tell me what has been happening in Fishtown these last months. Tell me what you know of the Russians—and of their plans."

"Aye, well." MacDougall rubbed at his eyes and shook his head slowly. "Fishtown's not what it was when you were last here. It's my wish the British Navy would show its flag more often on the coast, for if it did so the Russians would not have come."

"But now they *are* here—"

"Aye, it's too late, short of risking war. I follow what you said: that other ways have now to be found. It's a pity, but there's no use in crying over spilt milk."

"So I take it our interests have suffered?"

MacDougall nodded. "They have that. You spoke of— disappearences. They've happened, Mr Halfhyde, they've happened. Many of the traders and agents—"

"Including British?"

"Aye. Gone in the night, and in the morning no one the

wiser, and the Kroo bearers saying nothing. The story is put about that they've gone hunting up country, and come to grief, and never seen again." MacDougal gave a short laugh. "Those of us that are left know different!"

"The Russians?"

"Aye. It all started, d'you see, when that *Grand Duke Alexis* entered, some weeks ago. They're aboard there without a doubt, Mr Halfhyde."

"You're sure of this?"

"No, I'll not say I'm certain sure, it's guesswork, but I repeat, in my mind there's no doubt. Nor is there any doubt about the big guns they've landed, and set up in a battery overlooking us." MacDougall waved a hand north-eastward. "Four guns of heavy calibre they looked to me—the Russians brought them ashore from a cargo ship, a steamer, that came across the bar to anchor. They were winched on to floating pontoons and then manhandled from the jetty up into the jungle—a hell of a task, that was! Men died in the landing and in the hauling of them." He leaned towards Halfhyde, poking his pipe-stem towards the naval officer. "I'll tell ye, Mr Halfhyde, the bloody Russians have it in for us."

"But why?"

"Why?" MacDougall's eyebrows went up. "The trade, man, the trade!"

"Yes, I see that. But why shanghai the traders? What do they gain by that?"

The Scot shrugged. "You'd best ask them! Maybe it's just their way of doing business! It's effective: if a man's not at liberty, he can't trade; but if he's merely driven out of business, or dispossessed of his property and left to roam, why, then he can make trouble, even if only by spreading the word till one day it reaches London, or Lisbon, or wherever."

"As this has, though the shanghai element seems to have reached Gibraltar only. How did the news leave Fishtown, do you suppose?"

"Not by sea, Mr Halfhyde, seeing as no flag has been allowed contact with the shore, bar the Russian. I don't know the answer to that, I can only guess."

"Well?"

"It could be that not all the traders were shanghaied soon enough. One could have left Fishtown for a British trading post higher up the coast."

"But you don't know for certain?"

MacDougall sighed and said, "I told you, change has come to Fishtown. There is fear, much fear of what may happen. Thus, d'you see, there is no talk. If any man had decided to get out, he'd never say."

"Not even to a close friend?"

"No. Not even that. He would simply go, saying nothing, and with no need to say anything. There would be no complications, no household to arrange matters for. You know well, Mr Halfhyde, none of us traders have wives or families to bother with." The Scot smiled with a touch of wryness. "Hence the excellent business done by the Senhora, with whose trade not even Prince Gorsinski, I dare say, would seek to interfere!"

"Nor with yours either, Mr MacDougall?" Halfhyde asked, lifting an eyebrow. "With you, it seems to be business as usual."

MacDougall laughed. "Women and whisky are needed by all men."

"And you're still the sole importer from Scotland?"

"Aye, I am that, and have many friends among the distillers still too. They'd not supply any interlopers, Mr Halfhyde, and the Russians know that, I believe—or anyway, that's my hope— and they prefer the whisky to the vodka any day."

"But you could still be at risk?"

"I could, of course. No man's wholly certain these days, not even me."

Halfhyde drummed his fingers on the cloth-covered table, and listened absently to the thunderous beat of the rain on the roof. He looked at MacDougall searchingly. He asked, "Are you willing to take a risk in the interest of restoration of proper trade, Mr MacDougall . . . the risk of helping me, which will include the risk of giving me and Mr Runcorn shelter here, perhaps for longer than just tonight?"

MacDougall said, "Aye, I am willing. God be with your efforts, Mr Halfhyde." He held out a leathery hand, and took Halfhyde's in a firm grip.

They slept for what remained of the night, not in the beds as promised earlier, but on piles of old sacking, well hidden in MacDougall's stock-room behind crates of whisky, knowing that a search must come. When it did come, after warning by the guinea-fowl, they were ready for it, with Senhora da Luz's pistols cocked and MacDougall himself standing behind the Russian officer in charge of the search party, waiting his moment to strike. If anything looked like being uncovered, the searchers would die before they had a chance either to arrest or run: that, MacDougall had sworn on his oath. But bloodshed proved unnecessary. The search was perfunctory, a mere obedience to the order that all of Fishtown was to be gone through as quickly as possible. The thought processes of the Russian officer's mind were clear in his demeanour: he did not believe any mutineers would risk remaining in the town, but would have melted into the jungle country beyond in an attempt to get as far as possible from any seaport at all. When they had gone, MacDougall came back into the stock-room. "You'll not need to worry now," he said. "They've drawn this street and they'll not come back. I suggest you move to more comfortable quarters—I have camp beds that can be rigged in my living-room."

During the following afternoon, MacDougall left his store, making his \way down to the waterfront when for a space the torrential downpour had suspended itself as if to gather fresh strength for a new onslaught. He was gone for some while. When he returned, he reported that the *Grand Duke Alexis*, now wearing the Admiral's flag, and the *St Petersburg*, both appeared to be in normal routine though there was much coming and going of boats. The *Grand Duke Alexis* had, MacDougall believed, shifted her anchorage, moving a little farther out, presumably so as to keep clear of the shattered wreckage of the *Romanov*, whose remains were probably widely dispersed after the explosions.

"Any news of Prince Gorsinski?" Halfhyde asked.

"I spoke to a friendly officer," MacDougall said. "He's alive and in command of the squadron. That," he added, "was all I *did* learn. I thought it best not to seem to pump too obviously. What do you mean to do now, Mr Halfhyde?"

Halfhyde smiled, and caught the midshipman's eye. "What think you, Mr Runcorn?"

"Me, sir? I don't know, sir. Except that it's up to us to rescue the traders, sir . . . isn't it?"

"Well said, Wart—it is! Or it will be, once we know for certain they're there. If and when we do, Mr Runcorn, we go into action and damn the consequences, for the Russians will be seen to have committed what amounts to an act of war . . . at any rate, that will be how I'll propose to interpret it."

"And damn the consequences to your own career?" Mac-Dougall broke in, grinning.

"A career is a fragile flower at best, Mr MacDougall, and very often a dash of the unorthodox is the finest manure of all"

"Aye, if successful!"

"Well, we'll certainly not talk of failure. Let us talk of the *means* of action, shall we?" Halfhyde moved across to the window of the living-room, which opened to the rear of the store and gave a view of the jungle beyond the town. "Last night we spoke of the battery mounted by the Russians. I need to carry out a reconnaissance Mr MacDougall, and I've a feeling it needs to be done quickly. Tonight's as good a time as any."

Chapter 13

"YOU'LL need a guide," MacDougall said for the hundredth time. It was 2 A.M., and Halfhyde was ready to proceed. "I tell you—"

"Save your breath, friend," Halfhyde interrupted, running a finger along the blade of one of Senhora da Luz's knives; he found it razor sharp. "You've done enough, and I shall not accept more. Mr Runcorn and I are birds of passage, but your life is here. If the worst happens . . ."

"You were not going to talk of failure, I thought?"

Halfhyde grinned. "No more I am! But the possibility has to be thought of, and since it's there, I'm not going to risk compromising a good friend." He put a hand on MacDougall's shoulder. "It's not entirely an unselfish decision. You provide my base, and a good seaman always preserves his base whatever happens! I'll be back, never fear." He turned to Runcorn, who was armed with the pistols from the brothel and a knife pushed into the waistband of his trousers, while Halfhyde himself had the revolver from the officer aboard the *Romanov*, since dried out and cleaned by MacDougall. "Come on, Wart. Are you ready?"

"Yes, sir."

Smiling, Halfhyde looked him over. "The perfect warrior, bristling with arms . . . even the ferocious look in the eye! How d'you do it, Wart?"

"I don't understand, sir?"

"Well, never mind, never mind! You're a trifle scared, aren't you, Wart?"

"Oh no, sir!"

"Oh *yes,* sir, you are, sir! And why not, sir? I'm scared, damn scared, I can tell you! Do you know the best antidote to fear, Wart?"

"No, sir?"

"Then I'll tell you. In your case, a thought of Captain Fitzsimmons."

"Sir?"

"Does Captain Fitzsimmons scare you, Mr Runcorn? Or come to that, any other Post Captain in Her Majesty's fleet?"

Runcorn nodded. This was a proper fear to confess to. "Yes, sir!"

"And the Board of Admiralty scares me, with their power to project me back to Mrs Mavitty."

"Mrs Mavitty, sir?" Runcorn stared.

"Yes, Mrs Mavitty. Wart, there are worse things in life than the enemy. That's the whole basis of naval and military discipline. No man who fears his captain more than the enemy will ever run from a fight, no matter how hot it is. So bear Captain Fitzsimmons in mind, Mr Midshipman Runcorn, or if you prefer it, think of Mr Dalrymple-Martin. They are breathing down your neck, and Mrs Mavitty is breathing down mine. All right?"

"Er . . . yes, sir."

"Then we'll be away. And making more than a simple reconnaissance after all, for I've persuaded myself to believe in that report of British traders being held aboard the *Grand Duke*

Alexis. We won't wait for proof. Instead, Mr Runcorn, we shall take the fort."

"On our own, sir?"

"No. We're going to join the mutiny, Mr Runcorn, and enlist the help of Russian seamen against the Czar of all the Russias. Then we shall bring the guns of the fortress to bear on Prince Gorsinski's squadron—or what's left of it!"

"But sir . . . you said you disliked mutiny."

"I shall steel myself," Halfhyde said gravely, "with thoughts of Mrs Mavitty, and Camden Town."

Many miles to the south-westward as a murky dawn came up over Africa, the waking bugles blew along the spotless but fuggy mess decks of the *Aurora,* calling the off-watch hands from their hammocks as once again the cruiser steamed into the rendezvous area. In the slipstream of the bugles came the bosun's mates with their shrill calls and their time-honoured cries of "Show a leg, show a leg there, rise an' shine, the sun's a-burning yer eyes out!" Grumbling seamen and stokers looked down blearily, mouthing various obscenitites until the sharper orders of the ship's police brought them fast from the hammocks to begin another day's routine, to wash and clean, to lash up hammocks and stow them neatly in the netting, and have their breakfasts before falling in for Divisions, when they would be subjected to the stern appraisal of their officers. Inaction hung heavily upon the men. Going to sea was all very fine, it was what they had joined for, and it was better than being a barrack-stanchion in the dockyard hulks at Portsmouth or Chatham or Devonport; but this pointless cruising up and down outside the Gulf of Guinea, with a daily shift closer inshore, and no word of real explanation from the Captain or Commander or anyone else, left them restless and dissatisfied, and a prey to mess deck rumour and the galley telegraph. That there was some unspecified involvement with the Russians had come down to them from the Captain's pantry, via his servant and his servant's confidant, the petty officer of wardroom stewards. This, and the mysterious dropping off at sea of a lieutenant and a midshipman on a baulk of timber, had the lower deck agog; and after breakfast that morning the Commander reported as much, not for the first time, to Captain Fitzsimmons in the cuddy.

"We should give them some information, sir. They're all at sixes and sevens as it is."

"Is the fact affecting their efficiency, Commander?"

"Certainly not their efficiency, no, but—"

"Then I see no reason to divulge any information. A time will come, but it has not come yet." Fitzsimmons paused, pulled at his beard. "The Admiralty is particularly anxious that nothing should come out in the event of any *failure* on Halfhyde's part. Do you understand me, Commander?"

"I understand the need for a proper secrecy, sir, of course. But . . ."

"Come on, man! But what?"

"I understood, sir, that if Halfhyde should, as you put it, fail, then we were to enter the Bight and—"

"And show the flag?"

"More or less, sir. Even, if necessary, to prevent the sailing of the Russians."

"Then," Fitzsimmons said carefully, "I think you misunderstood the orders. I was left with full discretion to act, as I thought fit according to my assessement of any situation that might arise. Certainly there was a suggestion that in certain circumstances my ship might need to act preventively, but I have to bear in mind the overriding concern of the Admiralty that I should not provoke a crisis with Russia. Besides, the situation itself has changed—as we have known, indeed, since Gibraltar."

"The presence of Prince Gorsinski?"

Fitzsimmons nodded. "Exactly. And the fact of there now being three ships on the coast rather than just one."

"We knew this," the Commander pointed out, "before Halfhyde went overboard."

"So did Halfhyde, Commander, so did Halfhyde! If he should fail . . . well, I think he fully understood the risks involved."

The Commander's face was stiff. "I hope this doesn't mean he's going to be left to face the music, sir, while we remain outside? Surely the Admiralty could never have intended that?"

"The Admiralty's intentions are often left vague. It's up to the unfortunate Captain to make his interpretation. One day, perhaps not so far ahead, Commander, this new-fangled wireless telegraphy will be installed in the ships of the Fleet. Until it is,"—Fitzsimmons threw up his hands—"the decision is mine alone. Let us wish Halfhyde and Runcorn every success, and trust that they will be in contact soon."

Leaving MacDougall's store, wearing dark clothes provided by the Scot, Halfhyde and Runcorn headed east towards the back of the township, avoiding the occasional armed Russian patrol trudging along in the soaking downpour. Knowing the district as he did, Halfhyde had little difficulty with his bearings in spite of the night's almost total darkness; nor did he find it difficult to avoid the naval patrols. With the midshipman at his side he headed for jungle country, following directions given by McDougall, and reaching, after some two miles of difficult progress through the mud and rain, a track leading to the north from the jungle fringe. From this point they pressed along between the close-growing trees, shielded now to some extent from the rain's onslaught, but plunging deep into the mud brought by the previous day's permeations, swatting at mosquitoes, pushing aside branches and the twisting fronds of rubbery plant growth winding across the track from tree to tree.

According to MacDougall, they would reach the gun emplacement, which was protected by a strong wooden stockade, at the end of a three-mile walk along the track. The track itself, MacDougall had told them, opened into a jungle-ringed clearing on rising ground that gave the guns excellent cover of the anchorage and the coast around Fishtown.

"As protection for a naval base, yet to be established fully as such?" Halfhyde had asked.

"Aye, that's what I believe, and so, I don't doubt, does the Admiralty."

Halfhyde had not commented on this, remembering the admonitions of the Whitehall Rear-Admiral. But he had thought a good deal about the point made. If the Russian intent was indeed, as again the Admiralty had suggested, the establishment of a base with the direct intent of interfering with the British sea route to the Cape, then surely there was in that alone an inherent threat of war? British shipping could not be interfered with under conditions of peace, that was sure enough! The war might not come yet; it might not come for many years, perhaps, but that it lurked in the background Halfhyde did not doubt. Prince Gorsinski and his squadron were the pioneers for the future, and as such they had to be eroded away. Halfhyde gave a sudden shiver: once again, his thoughts had taken a turn towards the possible machinations of the Admiralty. Much might safely be blamed on an impetuous lieutenant and a deserting midshipman! He and Runcorn were far from immune against erosion themselves.

Forcing down such unwelcome fancies, Halfhyde pushed along the track, weary, dirty, soaked to the skin, flesh lacerated by the whipping branches and fronds which sometimes thwacked down agonizingly on the unhealed marks of the flogger's lash. It was a desperately slow progress and a dangerous one: at any moment they could have encountered a Russian armed party, though MacDougall had said the gunners manning the battery in fact used a shorter track giving direct access to the town and the jetty. Dawn was in the sky as they approached the clearing. In the faint lightening ahead, Halfhyde was able to make out the track's end. He halted, and put out a hand to Runcorn.

"Easy, Wart. Here begins the first reconnaissance. We'll take it slow. No sound, not the smallest. With bloody mutiny around them, the Russkies'll be alert to the drop of a pin."

"Yes, sir."

"In fact, I'll go ahead on my own from here, Wart. I'll not be long. He brought out his Russian revolver and drew back the hammer. "Fade into the trees and lie low."

"Yes, sir. And if anyone comes along, sir?"

"They won't. But if they do, keep out of sight—no heroics!"

Losing no time, Halfhyde went ahead, slow and quiet, using

previously learned bush-craft to keep all movement hidden. The dawn was a filthy one, as foul as the night, rain-filled and with heavy cloud hanging low—he was virtually in that cloud as he came, after another quarter of a mile or so, to the edge of the clearing. Keeping motionless in the trees, he watched. He saw the high stockade with its sharpened stakes looking like a circle of tiger's teeth; between the stakes, fleetingly, he saw the flicker of a storm lantern; and rising above the sharp point of wood he saw the gun-barrels, four heavy-calibre, grey muzzles lifting out over Fishtown and its anchorage. Around the perimeter the ground had been trodden flat, though now it was a sea of mud, and facing Halfhyde was a gateway, tight closed with, he guessed, a strong bar set in sockets across the inside. As he watched, sentries came into view, one from each flank approaching the gate, in long gray coats with heavy skirts, and carrying shouldered rifles with long snaky bayonets. At the gate each man turned about without speaking, and marched back, wet and miserable, the way he had come.

"Wart!"

Halfhyde had stopped more or less where he had left Runcorn to vanish into the tangle of trees. Runcorn had done a good job. There was no sign of him until a voice came from a point a little ahead of Halfhyde.

"It's you, sir."

"Truly said, Wart. Come out!"

"Aye, aye, sir." The midshipman appeared, dragging himself clear of the clinging vegetation. He stood at attention, smartly but incongruously.

"Oh, stand easy!" Halfhyde said with a touch of irritation. "This isn't the quarterdeck, though by God I'm more than beginning to wish it were! I've found the stockade, Wart."

"Yes, sir. What shall we do, sir?"

"Well, for a start, we'll not attack by ourselves, since I can't see any hope of taking it. We'll have to look for the mutineers, Mr Runcorn, that's what!"

"Yes, sir," Runcorn said dubiously.

"You sound unhappy. Why?"

"Well, sir, do you really think they'll help us?"

"I do. Why not!"

"To fight against their own country, sir?"

Halfhyde smiled and shook his head. "I doubt if they've much love for Russia, or at any rate for her rulers, Wart. And don't forget, they're facing death as it is. They've sunk one of their own cruisers, they've killed their officers, they've put a prince of the blood off his own flagship. I can't imagine a worse plateful than that—can you?"

"Well . . . no, sir, I can't."

"And we can offer them a chance to go on living. It's in their own interest to have Gorsinski's squadron under the cover of gunfire, isn't it?"

"Yes, sir. But do you mean to offer them something like a safe conduct to England?"

"Hardly that," Halfhyde answered with a laugh. "I can't see Captain Fitzsimmons agreeing to embark Russian mutineers, nor the Admiralty welcoming an embarrassment of that sort! No, Wart, when they've helped us gain the fortress, they can leave again . . . make their way up country, carve out a new life somewhere, without worrying about Prince Gorsinski. At least, as I said, it gives them a chance, doesn't it?"

"If they see it that way, sir."

"It's up to me to make them. But first we have to find them."

Runcorn looked unhopefully around at the thick growth. The jungle seemed impenetrable for more than a few yards from the track. In there, having once fought a way in, men could remain hidden for as long as they might wish, living off the country. The mutineers would be lying very low and not showing themselves, if indeed they had lingered in the vincinity of Fishtown at all, which was, in Runcorn's view, unlikely enough. But Halfhyde seemed to have few doubts that contact would be made. "There are a lot of them," he said. "The chances are that the two of us can move faster. They'll have their wounded to look after, for one thing, and that always slows down a retreat."

"But which way shall we look, sir?"

Halfhyde pointed back along the way they had come. "There was another track off this one, Wart, leading eastwards. For my money they'll have kept to the tracks—sailors aren't much of a hand at jungle country, or anyway I'm not. For want of anything better, we'll try that one. We'll head for the east, and we'll head openly, as bold as brass! If we don't see them, we'll have to hope they see us. Come on, Mr Runcorn."

He set off briskly, with the midshipman behind him.

There were signs of recent passage along the track leading east, as Halfhyde could see in the increasing day's light as it filtered behind the torrential rain through the covering of tree tops, but any men who had come along this way could well be from Prince Gorsinski's search parties. Halfhyde, having this very much in mind, was not surprised when, after a little over an hour's march, by which time both he and Runcorn were covered in thick, stinking slime from head to foot, he heard sounds from ahead. He held up a hand to Runcorn, and gestured into the tangle beside the track. "In!" he said in a whisper. "Fast but quiet, and keep dead still when you're hidden."

They pushed into the trees, and lay as flat as possible on the ground, their guns and knives ready. The sounds came closer; there was some singing over the sounds of trampling feet. Through the leaves and branches Halfhyde saw the Russian naval uniforms, and the rifles, and heard the clink of what he took to be chain. Before the men disappeared along the track, he had also seen the unarmed sailors, the ones with their hands shackled behind their backs, the recaptured mutineers, largely bearded men looking defiant rather than hangdog.

He reached out to the midshipman. "Some for the flagship's yard-arms," he said. "But not many! I think we're on the right track, Wart."

When the Russian party had gone on to a safe distance, Halfhyde led the way out again, and they trudged on, wet and tired, and also hungry now. Their wet state brought attacks of the shivers; and they shivered for different reasons when from time to time poisonous snakes slithered across the track, wet and gleaming, with camouflage that made them hard to see in the poor light. At the day's end they had found no one, and the wart's stamina was giving out, though he made no complaint—in fact he protested when Halfhyde called a halt and said he was showing the strain.

"Oh, no, sir, I'm perfectly all right, sir."

"You don't sound it, and by God you haven't looked it for the last few miles, Wart. We may be on a fool's chase after all, too—and I don't want to wear you out for nothing."

"I'm all right, sir. Honestly!"

Halfhyde grunted. "Well, if the truth be told, I'm *not*. I feel in need of a comfortable wardroom chair, the wellbeing of my nice, dry, mess dress, and a glass of whisky brought by a cheerful, friendly wardroom servant who understands perfectly that the moment the whisky's down I'll be ready for another. But that's not the way to be looking at life just now, is it, Wart?"

"No, sir. I suppose not."

"But you do, the same as me?"

Mr Runcorn hesitated. "Well—yes, sir."

"Honestly said!" Halfhyde clapped him on the shoulder. "We're due for a rest, Wart, a longer one than we've been having till now, and we're going to have it. Can you climb trees?"

"Yes, sir."

"Good." Halfhyde, as the light faded with the usual tropical swiftness, looked aloft. "Very close-growing, some of those branches, and wide, I'll hack us both to find somewhere to wedge ourselves safely for an hour or two—safely enough to sleep, perhaps."

"Yes, sir."

"Right, then . . . *Oh, Christ!*"

Halfhyde staggered. Something had hit hard, slamming into the region of his kidneys, yet he had seen nothing moving. In the next split-second, a heavily built man seemed to rise from the very earth behind Runcorn. A thick, tattooed forearm went round the wart's mouth, squeezing hard, and at the same time Halfhyde, who had lurched sickly against a tree trunk, felt the prick of a bayonet in his back.

Chapter 14

NOT a word was said. Halfhyde and Runcorn, their arms held tight by their sides and their weapons removed, were forced off the track and into the cover of thick jungle. Some twenty yards in, they were halted by a deep-voiced command from the darkness: "Stop, Petrovich!"

The escort stopped, still holding fast to the British officers. For a while, all Halfhyde could hear was the heavy breathing of the man behind him. Then, as a circle of men closed in, there was a rustling from all around, and dimly through the thick blackness Halfhyde could make out the forms, the dirty once-white duck uniforms, of the Russian seamen. A face, bearded and with the sharp smell of chewed tobacco strong on the breath that came from it, was thrust into Halfhyde's.

"Who are you?" the man demanded in Russian. "Are you for us or against us?"

Halfhyde, answering in the man's own language, spoke coolly. "We are for you if you'll give us the chance to be, friend."

"You know who we are, then?"

"Yes, I know you are mutineers, protesters against tyranny."

"So?" There was a pause, then the man spoke again. "Yet you are not from the *Romanov*, I think. If you are from the *Grand Duke Alexis*, or the—"

"I am from neither," Halfhyde broke in, "yet in a sense I am from the *Romanov*. I shall be honest with you, since I ask your help. I am Lieutenant St Vincent Halfhyde, Royal Navy, formerly the prisoner of your Admiral, Prince Gorsinski."

A murmur came from the circle of Russians, a murmur of surprise and anger, though Halfhyde felt the anger was not in fact directed at himself. Then another voice came, a voice from a little farther off: "It is the Englishman who was flogged by the aristocrat Gorsinski."

The beard moved closer. "Is this so, Englishman?"

"It is very much so," Halfhyde replied. "For proof, if you wish it, when daylight comes, you can see the marks for yourself. Perhaps they'll confirm that I'm no friend of His Highness Prince Gorsinski. Perhaps those marks will help you to trust me."

"You, an Englishman?" There was scepticism in the voice. "Why should we trust you?"

Halfhyde shrugged. "Because we can be of mutual help in a danger which we all face now, the danger of death. Some way back along the path, my friend and I saw some of your seamen under escort. I've no doubt Prince Gorsinski has his flagship's yard-arms ready . . . but then, you know the fate that awaits you all, you don't need me to tell you about it. As for me, I've no doubt I, too, will die—or would, if Prince Gorsinski got his hands on me again, which he will not. Death, my friends, is avoidable—but not, I think, if you remain here."

"We shall not remain here, Englishman."

"Where will you go?"

"To the interior."

"A long way, a very long way to safety, with Prince

Gorsinski's loyal sailors behind you with guns and handcuffs! Wouldn't it be better if there was no pursuit?"

For a few moments there was complete silence. Halfhyde sweated, sent up a prayer that these men might listen to him. After a while, the bearded man said, "Pursuit is certain, except, perhaps it can be avoided by one means."

"Yes?"

"We could hand you over, Englishman."

Halfhyde gave a laugh that he hoped would sound confident and easy. "In return for a safe conduct from Prince Gorsinski? Don't you know your own Admiral better than that? I'd agree he'd dearly love to have me back, but not, I'll warrant, at the expense of letting mutineers get away! Just think, Friend, just consider exactly how enormous your crimes are. Is Prince Gorsinski going to offer a lieutenant and a midshipman of the Royal Navy to the court of St Petersburg, as recompense for the burning of a Russian cruiser and the murder of her officers? Come now! It's your necks your Admiral wants, and only a fool would doubt it!" Into the silence that followed, Halfhyde dropped his offer. "Help me take the guns of the fortress that commands the town and the anchorage, and I'll guarantee thereafter to stop any men landing from the *Grand Duke Alexis* and the *St Petersburg*."

For men facing certain death if they should be taken, Halfhyde's offer was a good one, and Halfhyde was a persuasive talker. Nevertheless, it took him the greater part of that uncomfortable, rain-soaked and mosquito-bitten night to achieve agreement. Some of the men saw him as their best bargaining counter still; others, the majority, saw any action against the gun battery as likely to lead only to a worsening of their situation, and seemed disinclined to accept Halfhyde's breezy assurance that they could die only once. It was, Halfhyde insisted eloquently, quite impossible to make matters worse; thus, anything must be for the better. It was a constant repetition of this that at last penetrated stubborn minds, minds that in fact had no desire ever again to serve aboard a warship or to come within the gambit of Russian autocracy even if the miracle of a pardon should be accorded them. There was no talk of patriotism: these men had had enough, had suffered more despotic cruelty and privation than any human being should be called upon to face as a free man. They spat at the name of Gorsinski, at the name of the Czar, at mention of the court at St Petersburg. They spoke of growing, smouldering hatred among the rank and file of the Russian forces, of flame that would one day burn not only a single cruiser but the entire Russian fleet. There was talk aboard the ships, they said, that the best treatment for the pigs of officers was to feed them alive into the furnaces or to throw them into deep water with fire-bars tied to their feet.

"Drastic treatment," Halfhyde murmured. He felt in his bones that he had won; now, he wanted nothing so much as to try to sleep, to refresh himself and Runcorn for the next day's fight to gain the guns. "Do they really warrant that sort of end?"

"That, and worse if possible." The man who had spoken spat noisily. "Are you not worried in your Navy, that one day the men may strike back at you?"

"Not in the least," Halfhyde said with a laugh. "Our men are well-treated. They're content enough although they're given to grumbling."

"But the officer caste?"

"You can leave me out of that," Halfhyde interrupted. "I'm a man of the people. My one naval ancestor was of the lower deck like yourselves, a gunner's mate at Trafalgar."

That simple statement of fact, Halfhyde was to reflect later, set the seal upon his acceptance by the mutineers. There was a decided reaction to it: gasps and mutterings—such a thing was scarcely believable, that any gunner's mate should give rise to an officer of wardroom rank! Many, indeed, openly jeered in their disbelief; but Halfhyde was conscious of a friendliness from the more thoughtful of the Russians, and especially from their leader, one Yuri Reznichenko, who as it turned out had himself been a gunner's mate aboard the ill-fated *Romanov,* and who, because of his petty officer status, might well receive harsher treatment than the common seamen before the death sentence was carried out. Talking to this man, Halfhyde obtained his final confirmation that British nationals were being held aboard the *Grand Duke Alexis.*

"For what purpose?" he asked.

"That, I can't say, but it's to do with the trade."

Halfhyde nodded. "What's going to happen to them, when the *Grand Duke Alexis* sails again for Russia? Will they be taken too, or released?"

"The rumour is that they will be taken to Russia, though why, I don't know."

Halfhyde made a guess. Inside Russia, they wouldn't be able to talk. Written off already as lost on those up-country hunting expeditions, they had little hope . . .

Soon after this Halfhyde slept, together with Runcorn and Yuri Reznichenko, who offered them a share of a tarpaulin he had managed to bring ashore with him. Rain continued to fall for most of the night, cascading down the tree trunks and branches. If they came through this without a fever, Halfhyde thought as he woke at dawn, they would be the luckiest of men. He noted, as he got up from the tarpaulin, that Runcorn was suffering an attack of the shivers. He stretched, and stared up at the tree tops where the first faint lightening was just visible.

Soon, as the daylight began to increase, he was able to take a look at his companions. Reznichenko had told him already that his particular group was made up of a mixed bunch of seamen and stokers, eighty-seven in all. The rest of the ship's company, or such of them as had not been apprehended by Gorsinski's patrols, would, he assumed, be somewhere in the jungle around or making their way further inland. They could perhaps make contact with some of them; but Halfhyde, deciding that eighty-seven men, most of whom were armed with good sharp bayonets, though not with any rifles, should be ample for his purpose, said that speed was now the essential thing.

"We'll make the fort by sundown," he said, "if we don't get stuck in the mud on the way! You'll act as my petty officer?"

Reznichenko nodded. "I will."

Halfhyde held out a hand. "Then, as my petty officer, will you be good enough to let me have my Russian revolver back? And also give the knives and pistols to my midshipman? We shall need them, in our collective defence."

Slowly Reznichenko drew the revolver from inside his clothing and handed it, butt first, to Halfhyde. "Thank you," Halfhyde said as he took it. "I appreciate your trust, Petty Officer Reznichenko. Muster the men, if you please, and take the rear yourself with two men you can rely on implicitly, since we may

face trouble from any who're not fully converted." He gave the
Russian a long look. "Do you understand me?"

"Yes, I understand, but we are all in this together now, and
you need not worry."

"Right—I won't!" Halfhyde smiled, then caught the midshipman's eye. "Mr Runcorn?"

"Sir?"

"You'll march with me, at the head of the column. Eyes
skinned for Prince Gorsinski's patrols."

"Aye, aye, sir."

"As for breakfast, if we find any en route, well, then we'll
eat it. I've no doubt we'll find the fortress well provisioned for
supper. Petty Officer Reznichenko?"

"Yes?"

"Move out as soon as you're ready, if you please."

Reznichenko met his eye, recognizing the look and sound
of authority. With a curious mixture of respect and reluctance,
the Russian came to attention, then saluted smartly. His face
solemn, Halfhyde returned the salute with equal smartness. He
had scored a point and he knew it. He would be accorded loy-
alty and obedience. For his part, he would never let these men
down, whatever his personal feelings about the act of mutiny,
anathema to the British Navy in which it had not occurred since
the trouble at Spithead and the Nore almost a century earlier—
and then only because dishonest pursers had retained large
portions of the sailors' pay, a fair enough reason for dissatis-
faction among men who, even in refusing orders, had never put
their officers' lives at risk. Halfhyde was now in the company
of murderers and shipwreckers, but he would honour his part
of the bargain to the full.

• • •

It was a terrible march, under much worse conditions than the day before. The rain, though it ceased during the morning, had turned the track into a quagmire in which the men slipped and fell, cursing roundly. For many of them it was a bitter enough experience to be marching back towards the Russian ships instead of putting more distance between themselves and their princely oppressor. They were not slow to make this point, loudly and constantly, until Reznichenko enforced silence by lurid threats. They were, he said, committed to the English lieutenant; in his service lay their salvation, or at any rate their initial escape route. Muddily they struggled on, footsore, tired, hungry. They came upon wild berries from time to time, but mostly Halfhyde identified them as poisonous; and there was a sad lack of fruit. Halfhyde allowed two rests of half an hour's duration each so that the Russians could lie flat and gasping, spreadeagled on the sodden vegetation. There was a wild look in their eyes as they struggled back on their feet after these rests. Halfhyde, moving with words of encouragement down the line as they neared the end of the trail, found the looks growing wilder; these men, knowing only too well what was at stake, would fight passionately and to the end.

In fact a foretaste of their capabilities, though not at first noticed in Reznichenko's reaction, came when the head of the column was within half a mile of the point where the track joined the one leading from the town to the fortress. The beat of a drum was heard, distantly, giving a step, probably down in the streets of Fishtown. Reznichenko called to Halfhyde, "A patrol!"

"And coming nearer," Halfhyde said after a few moment's

listening. "Into the trees with all hands, Petty Officer Reznichenko!" When they were all hidden, he conferred with the Russian gunner's mate. "Their arms will come in handy. Are you willing to attack, if they come up this way?"

Reznichenko scowled, wiping the back of a hand across his bearded face. "If they're seamen, they're our own kind."

"So will be the soldiers in the fort."

"But different! Soldiers are more for the aristocrats than we seamen. And they'll be from our own ships—our friends, who but for chance might have mutinied themselves. No, we'll not attack. We'll let them go by."

"It's your life, Reznichenko, remember that. And your men's lives."

Reznichenko shook his head. "If we let them go by, they'll not see us. There's no danger in that."

Halfhyde met his eye, read the final decision, and gave way gracefully. He shrugged. "Very well, it's up to you. No attack." Though he could find no quarrel with the Russian's sentiments, he regretted leaving much-needed rifles and ammunition to walk peacefully by and away. That would be a bitter sight to see!

Some minutes later the approaching but still distant drumbeat ceased, no doubt as the possibility of keeping step vanished in the slither of mud. More time passed. Then the rattle of equipment and rifles could be heard plainly. The patrol was coming up their track, would pass right by them.

In dead silence, they waited, eyes peering through cover, bodies motionless. The seamen went by in single file, rifles held across their mud-spattered bodies, slipping and lurching on the thick slimy layer, their officer in the rear with a hand on the butt of a holstered revolver. Halfhyde watched that officer's face, read the latent sadism in thin, tight-drawn lips, the arrogance in the set of the head, the fastidiousness that disliked a muddy uniform . . . and then, horrifyingly, he saw the officer's expression change like a striking snake, saw the glitter in the eyes, and realized that by some wicked chance their eyes had met and the officer was aware of a man in the trees.

The revolver came out in a flash; the officer shouted out to the patrol, who swung round with their rifles. A bullet zipped past Halfhyde's head, lodging in a tree trunk, to be followed by a barrage of rifle-fire, and then by the cries of wounded men. By now the whole picture had changed. The mutineers, fired upon blindly, came storming out in a vicious fighting mood.

Reznichenko himself snatched Halfhyde's Russian revolver, aimed it at the officer, and fired. The officer went down, his skull shattered, blood and brains drooling into the mud. The men of the patrol continued firing, and this act alone decided their end. Yelling, screaming obscenities, the mutineers went in hard with the naked steel of the bayonets, thrusting, twisting, and withdrawing, using fists and feet, slashing, cutting. Grossly outnumbered, the patrol had no chance. Within three minutes of the first shot it was over, with not one man of the patrol surviving. Halfhyde, breathing hard, registered that it was about the most savage thing he had ever seen, and the most efficient piece of killing. There had been no comradeliness shown on either side.

Reznichenko put it into words. "They were not for us," he said simply. "They all had to die." Without orders from Halfhyde, he set the mutineers to drag the bodies into the jungle, and when they were all well hidden and the blood stirred into the mud, he made a count of heads. The mutineers had lost only three men dead, and suffered five more wounded in varying degrees. And among them they now had one more revolver and twelve rifles.

"And not far short of twelve hundred rounds of ammunition," Reznichenko reported.

Halfhyde responded absently. "Yes. And a drum!"

"A drum?"

"A drum to give the beat . . . to a patrol, Petty Officer Reznichenko! Don't you see?"

A look of happy dawning spread over the Russian's face. "A patrol! We march into the fort . . . as a patrol."

"Aye, a patrol that has made a good haul of mutineers, marching in to the beat of the drummer—it can't fail! Arm twelve men, if you please, Reznichenko, and fall the rest in between them. Quickly, now!"

Chapter 15

THEY marched in single file where the track was narrow, with the armed men in front and behind; when the track broadened beyond the intersection, Halfhyde changed the formation, and they went ahead openly and as fast as possible, as full dark came down, with the supposedly recaptured mutineers marching with their armed escort on the flanks. Halfhyde went ahead now, with Runcorn; in the rear was Reznichenko. In front of Halfhyde, a drummer beat out the step, the captured side-drum moving against his thigh. It was a difficult march in the total darkness, but soon enough Halfhyde made out the glimmer of light ahead in the clearing, the flicker of the storm lanterns behind the sharply pointed stockade. Halting the advance, he turned and moved down the line of the Russians a little way before the end of the track.

"Remember," he said, "I ask for the gates to be opened. As soon as they open up, we march straight in. We'll not know the situation until we're inside. I shall make a quick appraisal. There will be no shooting until I give the word. When I do give it, you must, for your own sakes, make a good job of it. I'm sure you all realize that we can't risk failure," He turned away. "Mr Runcorn?"

"Sir?"

"This'll be your first taste of action. Keep your head and use your eyes."

"Yes, sir."

"And watch your back as well. You'll have been taught fair play at your prep school, and in the *Britannia* too. Forget it— for as sure as God's in His Heaven, the Russians will! All right, Mr Runcorn?"

"Yes, sir."

Halfhyde smiled, invisibly in the darkness, and reached out a hand. "Good luck, Wart. Just do your best, that's all."

"I will, sir. Thank you, sir." There was the movement of a salute, vaguely seen, and the midshipman turned about and went back to his place at the head of the line. Halfhyde followed, then gave the order to march again to the drummer's beat. They moved on briskly, entering the clearing, still seeing the storm lanterns' light inside the stockade, and coming within range of the sentries. As the once-white uniforms loomed through the dark behind the drum's tattoo, one of the sentries, facing them with his rifle levelled, called on them to halt.

Halfhyde gave the order, and the drum fell silent. Halfhyde could almost feel the tension coming like a physical force from the men behind him.

"Who goes there?" the sentry called out.

"Friend."

"What friend?"

"A patrol from Prince Gorsinski's squadron—from the *Grand Duke Alexis,* with mutineers from the *Romanov.*"

"Advance and be recognized."

His heart seeming to beat like the side-drum itself, Halfhyde ordered the seamen to advance, halting them again within a circle of yellow light from the guard lantern at the gate. He said shortly, "I am a lieutenant of the Imperial Navy, and not to be kept waiting. The gate, man! Have it opened at once." When the soldier appeared hesitant, Halfhyde went on, "There was fighting—my uniform was torn away. I have desperate men, and no wish to continue down to the jetty in darkness. I say again, open the gate, or there will be trouble."

Halfhyde's harsh, authoritative tones produced a good effect. The sentry saluted, nodded towards his companion, who beat with his rifle-butt on the stout wood of the gate and shouted for entry for the naval party. The waiting men heard sounds as of a bar being lifted from sockets, and then the gate was swung open from inside. At once Halfhyde gave the order to advance, and the party marched in smartly. And watchfully.

Halfhyde, sweeping his glance around the fort's wide expanse of mud, saw the great guns on their mountings, heavy field pieces lie. of their limbers, and a guard running to muster outside a kind of gatehouse which no doubt acted as a guardroom. From beyond the guns came two officers, in high boots that shone with polish where the mud was not, and wearing epaulettes: a major and a captain of artillery.

"What's this?" the major demanded, raising thin sandy eyebrows at Halfhyde.

Halfhyde bowed, hiding the glint in his eyes. He had debated much with himself as to whether he should carry on the deception and then strike when the fortress personnel had their guard lowered, but had decided against the risks of premature exposure inherent in such a plan. Having made his polite bow, he straightened and caught the eye of Reznichenko. "Open fire!" he shouted.

There was nothing lacking in the mutineers' response. Those who were armed at once turned their rifles and bayonets against the gate guard, who, taken completely by surprise, were mown down to a man to lie dead or mortally wounded in the clinging mud inside the gate. Others took the rifles from the fallen men and on Reznichenko's order ran outside to deal with the two sentries. Halfhyde flung himself bodily at the nearer of the two Russian military officers, the captain, while Runcorn took exemplary charge of a body of mutineers, and charged towards the major and more troops running out behind him.

It was a furious fight, with neither side showing any mercy. Halfhyde, struggling with the captain of artillery, saw Reznichenko thrust a bayonet right into the throat of a sergeant; bloodily, the tip protruded from the back of the neck before Reznichenko pulled it out again. The sailors were fighting mad, with all at stake, and the fort's defenders, outnumbered in any case, had no chance. Halfhyde threw the artillery captain from him in a tremendous heave, to land him in a heap at the foot of the stockade. As the Russian officer fell, a sailor swung a bayoneted rifle at him and plunged the steel deep into his stomach. After that, Halfhyde metaphorically shut his eyes to the slaughter. As a man it sickened him, as an officer it appalled and horrified him, but he knew too well what these mutineers faced if they allowed any man to live. Within half an hour of the first shot it was all over: every man of the garrison lay dead or dying.

Reznichenko, with ten of his seamen and stokers dead, and many more with gunshot and bayonet wounds, took a party of men through the fort's living quarters and stores. Halfhyde heard more shots, a few cries; then Reznichenko came back to report the place clear.

"A bloody night's work," Halfhyde said sombrely.

"Bloody indeed, but you now have the guns." Smiling, the Russian waved an arm towards the great gun-barrels. "You have command of the port and the anchorage, Englishman, if I care to give it to you."

"And do you, Petty Officer Reznichenko?"

Reznichenko gave a quiet laugh, and for a few moments studied the British lieutenant's face in the light from a lifted storm lantern against the glass of which the rain sliced like a curtain. "I do. I keep my word. I have no use for the guns. All I want is time, Englishman, time to get away from the aristocrat Gorsinski. You have said you will give me this, and I trust you."

"Why such trust?" Halfhyde asked.

Reznichenko shrugged. "You are an English officer. All the world knows that English officers do not break their promises."

"Thank you for that," Halfhyde said quietly. "I shall not let you or your men down, you may depend upon it." His tone became brisker. "Now to the more immediate future. I shall not attempt to make contact with your flagship until tomorrow daylight. In the meantime, we must take into account the possibility of more searches by Prince Gorsinski. In case any search parties come by the fort, we shall need sentries dressed as soldiers."

"That will be arranged," Reznichenko said.

"Well, Mr Runcorn, there's greater comfort here than in the jungle. Russian officers have never been noted for frugal living, but I hardly expected to find this degree of luxury inside a simple stockade." Halfhyde looked around in the lamplight, rubbing his hands pleasurably. The major and the captain seemed to have brought all the comforts of home to the West African coast: a sumptuous carpet covered the boards of what had been their anteroom in a wooden building that also housed a small mess and two bedrooms, with kitchen and pantry; there were comfortable chairs, beautiful pieces of elegant furniture; there were occasional tables, a folding card table topped with green baize, an ornate fireplace with heavy steel fire-irons, and rich curtains over the two big windows. The place had a feeling of ease and opulence which contrasted strongly with the bare, damp barrack-room accorded the common soldiers, a room almost filled with seedy-looking bunks each with a single grey blanket, and little else. And, importantly, the officers' mess was nicely and liberally equipped with bottles of vodka, brandy, Scotch whisky, and excellent French wines.

"From MacDougall, no doubt," Halfhyde said, caressing a bottle of whisky. "No wonder they've never interfered with his trade! You'll join me, Mr Runcorn?"

"Well, sir . . ."

"Yes, you will. Officers need to learn drinking as they need to learn other aspects of their profession. A teetotal naval officer is a naval officer to be suspicious of, Mr Runcorn, for everyone has his vices—and a decent capacity for drink is an honest and an open vice! Glasses, Mr Runcorn, and water if you wish. Then we'll talk about tomorrow, while Reznichenko has a meal made ready."

Halfhyde sauntered back into the anteroom, carrying a lamp, and sat in one of the elegant walnut chairs. When Runcorn came in with the glasses, he poured the whisky, watching the golden glow with immense pleasure as it fell into shining crystal. He lifted his glass.

"To the guns, Mr Runcorn."

"The guns, sir."

They drank. Halfhyde, studying Runcorn, asked, "What's the matter, Wart?"

"The matter, sir?"

"You seem out of spirits."

"Me, sir? No, sir!"

"Yes, sir! You're tired; you're shivering. More whisky, Wart, and start to enjoy life again!" Crossing the room, Halfhyde refilled the midshipman's tumbler, then said, "At first light tomorrow, Mr Runcorn, you will go into Fishtown, alone."

"Aye, aye, sir."

"You will go direct to the foreshore and find a native crew willing to use their canoe to put you aboard the *St Petersburg*. If you're apprehended by a patrol before you reach the jetty, you'll say who you are, and that you are giving yourself up, and wish to see the Admiral. Clear?"

"Yes, sir."

"You'll make no mention of me, or of the mutineers. Or of the fort. Understand?"

"I understand, sir."

"You'll insist that it's your right to talk only to Prince Gorsinski. I don't think you'll have any trouble over that. You'll tell Gorsinski some of the facts, but not all. There is to be no mention of any mutineers, Mr Runcorn. We saw none, and we took the fort between us, you and I, after shooting the sentries."

"Do you think Prince Gorsinski will believe? . . ."

"No, Mr Runcorn, I don't, but I'm doing what little I can for Reznichenko and the others by telling no tales. As for Gorsinski, when you tell him the rest of your story, he won't be worrying too much about how the taking of the fort was achieved. The fact will be enough, at any rate so far as you are concerned. You'll simply go on to tell him the truth: that I have command of the guns, and I can sink his precious flagship at a moment's notice. And will do so if he doesn't surrender all foreign nationals held aboard the *Grand Duke Alexis*. And if you ask, as I see you're about to, if he'll believe *that,* then the answer's yes, he will. Because, Mr Runcorn, I shall be watching the foreshore through the gunner major's field glasses, and I shall see you leave. I shall see you board the flagship, and I shall give you fifteen minutes from that moment. When the fifteen minutes are up, I shall open fire. Just one round, to send a nice dollop of the Bight of Benin over Prince Gorsinski's decks. After that, you can tell His Highness he has one hour flat, no more and no less, in which to hand over the traders and give you a boat. If he doesn't, I'll open with all four guns of the battery, my point of aim being the hulls of his blasted squadron. Any questions so far?"

"Yes, sir." Runcorn, his eyes oddly bright and his face flushed, was sitting at the very edge of his chair. "Suppose Prince Gorsinski opens fire first, sir?"

"He won't. Not first. You'll tell him he's to keep his guns unmanned, and all hands off the upper decks of his ships. As soon as I see the first sign of a gun's crew moving to action stations, I'll open on the flagship, on which the whole battery will be ready laid and trained. No doubt he'll open later, but he'll never open first, Mr Runcorn! Once the traders are handed over, I'll simply have to fire faster, and more accurately, than Gorsinski, that's all!"

"And the traders, sir?"

"You'll take them out to sea in a south-westerly direction, Mr Runcorn."

"I, sir?"

"Yes, you, sir."

"But Prince Gorsinski, sir . . ."

"No, sir. Prince Gorsinski will not hold on to you, for if he does, that's another signal to me to open fire." Halfhyde wagged a finger at the midshipman. "Don't cross your bridges, sir! I'll give you cover out to sea, where you'll contact the *Aurora* in the daily rendezvous position and be picked up."

"And you, sir?"

"Don't worry about me," Halfhyde said. "Just tell Captain Fitzsimmons I expect him to wait for me. In due course, I'll turn up."

After a meal provided by Reznichenko, Halfhyde and Runcorn took watches turn and turn about, sleeping in their watch below. During his period of duty, Halfhyde, pacing up and down beside the guns, looking out over the anchorage and the lights of Prince Gorsinski's squadron, was restless in his mind, his thoughts racing. He was, he knew, about to commit an enormity, if Prince Gorsinski should force him to open fire on that squadron; about to throw finally to the winds his orders for discretion. But he saw no alternative, since the *Grand Duke Alexis* had British nationals aboard, a fact apparently unknown to the Admiralty, at any rate at the time he had been given his orders. In Halfhyde's view, this altered those orders and left him with the clear duty to use his knowledge and his initiative in the British interest. So much for that. He would act as he had decided and face the music later.

A more currently pressing anxiety concerned Reznichenko and the other mutineers. What of his promise to give them time to get away under cover of the guns? In that respect, some subterfuge had yet to be thought of. Halfhyde paced, frowning into the black night, thinking furiously but coming to no decision other than that he would not under any circumstances break his word to the trusting Russian sailors, though, if he was to give the men the clear start they needed, he would have to remain at his firing-post for a devil of a long time! On the other hand . . . there were, as ever, more ways than one of dealing with princes. A few well-placed shells from the shore battery might give Gorsinski more than a water-dousing with which to concern himself. Mutiny was a catching disease and there was no reason to suppose that the ships' companies of the *St Petersburg* and the *Grand Duke Alexis* would be slower than the men of the shattered *Romanov* to take an opportunity.

Halfhyde, his pace quickening with his thoughts, moved inside to call Runcorn for his watch, but, reaching the midshipman's bedside, and looking down in the light of a flickering lamp, he realized with a sense of shock that other diseases than mutiny could strike naval officers. Mr Midshipman Runcorn was obviously very sick.

Chapter 16

"I'LL be all right, sir It's nothing much."

"My good Wart," Halfhyde said, "you'll not be all right. Either for your watch or for bearding Prince Gorsinski. It's a damn nuisance but it can't be helped, and it's not your fault." He turned away, pacing the room, disregarding Runcorn's continuing protestations. The midshipman was in a bad way, shivering violently yet sweating like a pig. Halfhyde recognized the symptoms of malaria. Inwardly he cursed. The boy must remain in his bed, that was clear, and without a medical man he might very well die in any case. Gorsinski had doctors in his ships, but Gorsinski was unlikely to sanction their being sent ashore. If Runcorn was allowed to go ahead with the plan, he might get attention once he was aboard. Halfhyde rejected this the moment it came into his mind. The carrying out of the plans could not be left in the hands of a sick midshipman, nor could Halfhyde send a sick midshipman out into the rains and a long trek to the jetty. To do that would be murder. Savagely, Halfhyde damned his filthy luck in a lengthy but silent monologue; then, doing his best to maintain an untroubled and confident face, he turned back to the wart, tossing and turning restlessly in the bed.

"Sleep if you can," he said. "In any case, try not to worry. I shall cope. I'm going out now, to talk to Reznichenko. I dare say there are medicines—the Russians will have had malaria in mind. We'll have a look, and do all we can for you, Wart."

"Sir . . ."

"Yes?"

"I've messed everything up, sir."

"No," Halfhyde said. "I told you I'll cope. I also said, don't blame yourself. Blame the mosquitoes, and the filth they carry."

"Sir, the Captain . . ."

"Captain Fitzsimmons? What about him, Mr Runcorn?"

The midshipman, looking dazed, tried to answer but failed. Halfhyde fancied he was verging on delirium and blamed himself for not having realized earlier. Runcorn had been shivering before, had clearly been deathly cold, and at times languorous, with a general depression of his spirit; he was now in the first true attack of the disease, and probably with a very high temperature. Halfhyde went to the outer door and shouted for Reznichenko, then went back to the bed and laid a hand on the midshipman's sweating forehead. It was burning hot to the touch. Halfhyde gently wiped away the sweat with his handkerchief, only for more great beads to form. Turning away again, he hunted around the bedroom, opening cupboards and drawers, searching for medicines, finding none. A moment later Reznichenko came in and looked in concern at the tossing figure.

"Ah, Reznichenko!" Halfhyde swung round. "A change in the plans, I fear. As you can see, my midshipman is very sick, I believe with the malaria. God knows what we're going to do now, but the first thing is quinine. Will you be good enough to search the fort for quinine, Reznichenko?"

"I've already found quinine, during a general search."

"Well done! Bring it quickly, and a glass."

The Russian went off and was back within the minute with a bottle of quinine. Quickly Halfhyde poured a fair sized dose; no doctor, he could only guess at a quantity. This he held to Runcorn's lips, supporting his head and forcing the midshipman to drink. The result was a stream of vomit. When the spasm was over, Halfhyde poured another dose and this time it seemed as though it would stay down. The terrible shivering continued, and the face was still a nasty yellow-white, but there was nothing else that could be done.

Halfhyde looked at Reznichenko. "I'll have to go out in his place," he said. "Reznichenko, you're a gunner's mate. You're more than capable of taking charge here in the fort without me."

"Capable, yes."

"And willing?"

Reznichenko shrugged. "I think whether you are here or not here makes little difference. I and the others would have been needed to fire the guns if they had to be fired. I am willing, yes, but I am not the only one concerned."

"But they'll obey your orders?"

"We are mutineers, Englishman. Do mutineers obey orders?"

"I expect they do, when it's in their own interest to do so, Petty Officer Reznichenko. Which on this occasion it is. If you can't control them any longer as a petty officer, I think you can control them as a man. You don't seem to me to lack personal authority." Halfhyde stared into deep-set eyes that met his steadily and calmly. "I see character in your face, Petty Officer Reznichenko, character and confidence. For your sake and your men's, I ask you to use it. All my own promises stand, and I shall come back to pick up my midshipman when the time is right. Well?"

The Russian held his gaze. Then, giving a slight inclination of the head, he said sombrely, "Very well, Englishman, I shall see to it that the guns fire. Always, since agreeing to your plan, it has been understood what we would have to do. But one thing you must accept, and it is this: in the beginning we fire only to threaten, that is, shells that will fall over or short. There will not be killing unless it is necessary. You understand?"

"I think I do," Halfhyde said. "But if Gorsinski should send boats inshore, with armed patrols—what then?"

"Then we shall sink them," Reznichenko said.

Halfhyde, coming out from the track leading down from the battery, walked openly along Fishtown's waterfront under a short and welcome respite from the rain. In comparative clearness he could see the two Russian cruisers swinging to their anchors in the disturbed, seething waters of the anchorage, and, as he looked, he heard distantly the sound of the bugles as the Russian naval ensigns were hoisted slowly to the ensign staffs on the quarterdecks. Halfhyde smiled to himself, visualizing a high degree of watchfulness now on the part of the officers. He felt that Gorsinski must be a very rattled man; and, knowing the Admiral as he did, he was certain that Gorsinski's reaction would never be to use the soft pedal as a means of quietening any incipient trouble. Gorsinski's whole character and attitude was arrogant and domineering and his iron methods were wholly predictable.

As Halfhyde watched, a boat came into view, riding the surf in the distance, not unskilfully handled. The *Grand Duke Alexis,* from which ship the boat seemed to be coming, had been a long time on station, and her boats' crews had no doubt learned the local offshore seamanship better than the other vessels' sailors. Halfhyde watched the boat cross the sand bar in safety, if in discomfort, and make for the river jetty. There were more armed seamen abroad, another armed party on a hunt for the *Romanov's* mutineers, no doubt.

Fishtown itself was for the moment quiet, with no marching patrols to interfere with the natives as they busied themselves with their dug-out canoes along the foreshore. Halfhyde moved down the beach towards a group of fishermen around a large canoe. Halfhyde spoke to the man who appeared to be in charge, and who would, he said, take the white man out to the big ship in the anchorage. A little later, sitting in the canoe's stern and holding on for his life, Halfhyde ventured out across the breakers in the care of the native fishermen. It was a dangerous passage, but accomplished with the apparent ease and efficiency that his earlier sojourn in the Bight of Benin had led him to expect from the native canoe-handlers. His fears, as he was propelled out towards the flagship and past the water-swilled remains of the *Romanov,* visible in the ebb-tide, were not fears of seamanship. The uncomfortable feeling in the pit of his stomach was due to the proximity of the lion's mouth. He would be pretty firmly in Russian hands within the next half-hour. Everything now depended upon Reznichenko.

Aboard Her Majesty's cruiser *Aurora,* currently steaming north in the rendezvous area, the Officer of the Watch, pacing the bridge, stopped and listened, then used his telescope to look closely along a bearing to the north-west. There was no land in sight and no ships, but the sound he had heard had been unmistakable. He bent to the Captain's voice-pipe and blew down it. It was answered immediately.

"Captain, sir. There is gunfire to the north-eastward. One shot only, so far."

The voice rattled in his ear. "Gunfire, dammit? You're sure, Mr Cotterrell?"

"Quite sure, sir."

A pause. Then, "Can you identify it?"

"A heavy gun, sir. Too heavy, I believe, for any ship."

"The shore fortifications?"

"That seems more than likely, sir."

There was another pause, then the Captain's orders came up the voice-pipe: "Maintain your course and speed, Mr Cotterrell. Inform the Commander and the Fleet Engineer. I shall be up directly."

"Aye, aye, sir." Cotterrell replaced the polished brass cover of the voice-pipe and scanned the seas ahead of the cruiser's stem. The sea was clear but windswept, with breaking wave-tops below a heavily overcast sky that threatened to come right down to sea level with a consequent effect upon the visibility—unpleasant conditions under which to enter the Bight of Benin, if that was to be the Captain's decision. Awaiting the Captain, Cotterrell checked the ship's position by dead reckoning and laid it off on the chart.

Within two minutes, footsteps clattered on the bridge ladder and the gold oak-leaves of the Captain's cap appeared. Fitzsimmons stalked to the forward rail and stood for a few moments in silence, scanning the sea. Then he swung round on Cotterrell.

"How far to the northern limit of the rendezvous area, Mr Cotterrell?"

"Three miles, sir."

"Ah. Reduce the revolutions, Mr Cotterrell, if you please. The telegraphs to slow ahead."

"Aye, aye, sir. Slow ahead both engines," Cotterrell said, passing the order to a seaman boy. The telegraph handles were drawn right back, pushed forward again, and settled on Slow Ahead. Bells clanged, and the engine-room indicator moved in acknowledgement.

"Engines repeated, slow ahead, sir."

Fitzsimmons nodded. "Thank you, Mr Cotterrell. The helm fifteen degrees to starboard, and keep it there. I shall circle."

"Starboard fifteen, sir."

The quartermaster put the wheel over, chewing phlegmatically on a quid of tobacco. The *Aurora's* head swung off, and she began her circle while Captain Fitzsimmons reflected, deciding on his future course of action. For some ten minutes he remained staring out ahead at the restless grey sea, then he bent forward and called down to the deck below.

"Commander."

The Executive Officer, who had been talking to the chief gunner's mate, looked up and saluted. "Sir?"

"My cabin, if you please, at once."

"Aye, aye, sir."

Fitzsimmons turned to the Officer of the Watch. "I shall be in my cabin, Mr Cotterrell. I'm to be informed at once of any further gunfire, or of the sighting of any ship."

"Aye, aye, sir." Cotterrell hesitated. "Shall I continue circling, sir?"

"I have not countermanded that order, Mr Cotterrell, to the best of my knowledge, have I?"

"No, sir."

Fitzsimmons stalked to the ladder and went down, his rigid back seeming to register disapproval of an unnecessary question.

Gorsinski was in a rage, a flat fury. He was disbelieving that Halfhyde could have gained control of the shore battery, and the Englishman's impertinent assurance, coupled with his threats and demands, made the Admiral shake with anger. Halfhyde met with a tirade: he would be flogged again, he would be mastheaded, he would be broken, keelhauled until the barnacles ripped his flesh to shreds. In the middle of this outburst, Reznichenko played his part admirably. Precisely fifteen minutes after Halfhyde, visible through the gunner major's field glasses, had stepped upon the quarterdeck of the St Petersburg, the first warning shot came thundering from the battery, splashing down outside Prince Gorsinski's cabin ports to send up a mighty column of water that dropped back with a roar on deck above. Gorsinski stopped dead, in mid-bluster, and stood with his mouth open.

"I did tell you so," Halfhyde murmured.

"Great God."

"I doubt if He'll be found in a helpful mood. You now have one hour, sir—one hour only. May I—"

There was a loud banging on the door and the cruiser's Captain entered unceremoniously to report. "Your Highness, the ship is under fire, apparently from—"

"Kindly take some action, you fool!" Gorsinski's face was

livid, his hands trembling. "Sound the alarm at once—all guns' crews to close up and bear—"

"No," Halfhyde broke in, wagging a finger in Gorsinski's face. "You'll belay that order, my dear sir, forthwith, unless you wish to have your ship sunk under you! May I remind you of what I said when I came aboard. Your squadron is now helpless, with the shore guns ready laid and trained to bear upon both ships. The moment you close up *your* guns' crews, *my* guns will open fire. You, sir, are a sitting target, and believe me, there's nothing you can do about it except to agree to my terms. I advise you, sir, to accept defeat gracefully."

Gorsinski's eyes flashed, but he seemed uncertain now. He lifted his arms, shook them frustratedly in the air, his face almost purple. "I accept nothing!" he shouted. "Do you hear, nothing! I shall have you—"

"Consider, sir. Consider your position carefully. I say again, you have one hour. You should use that hour to the best effect." Halfhyde pointed through the port towards the shore. "Those guns, as you know well, are heavier than anything you possess, and they have you in their sights. You'll not be allowed to man your guns before they open on you. Whatever you do, sir, you can't avoid that now. Do you mean to lose your squadron, and provoke a war with the British Empire? Is that what the Czar wants, Prince Gorsinski?"

Gorsinski paced the cabin, back and forth, hands clasped behind his back. In the doorway, the Captain waited his orders. Behind him, Halfhyde could see the sentry with his rifle. It was, he knew, touch and go. Gorsinski was perhaps a man sufficiently ruled by his passions to take any risk rather than submit to threats, though in all conscience the risk surely outweighed any considerations such as the establishment of a trading station—*unless Russia did indeed intend war.* That was one of the imponderables, and represented a fifty-fifty risk to Halfhyde as well as to Gorsinski, a fact that seemed suddenly to dawn on the Russian, who stopped his pacing and turned to face Halfhyde squarely.

"And you, Lieutenant Halfhyde. Do you wish to provoke a war with my country? Is this what your Queen Victoria would wish, Queen Victoria with her family relationships at the court of Czar Nicholas?"

"If it is forced upon her," Halfhyde answered evenly, "I doubt if she'd shrink from a fight. In the meantime, I have committed no hostile act."

"Then taking a Russian outpost is not hostile?"

"Taking a Russian outpost that has no authority to be where it is, is not hostile—no."

"Words, words!" Gorsinski waved his arms again. "If you open fire on my ships, *then* you commit a hostile act."

"No, sir. I shall act only in the interests of the freedom of British subjects, confined by you aboard the *Grand Duke Alexis.* And to that, I think, you have no answer at all." Halfhyde, folding his arms, grinned into Gorsinski's angry face. "As you see, sir, I hold the best cards after all."

"You think so? Suppose I land armed seamen across the bar, to retake the fort? What then, Lieutenant Halfhyde?"

Halfhyde shrugged. "If a boat is seen leaving the ship, the effect will be the same as if you manned your guns, and," he said, raising his voice above Gorsinski's almost demented retort, "the boats themselves will be sunk before they reach the first line of surf."

Gorsinski seemed to swell physically, to fill the cabin with his fury. "Then I shall retake the battery later, when the time is right for me, Lieutenant Halfhyde. In the meantime, its guns can reach so far and no farther! I shall take my ships to sea, and place them outside the range of the guns." He turned on his new Flag Captain. "Bring in the escort, Captain Chernik. The prisoner is to be confined in cells and is to remain there if we should be fired upon."

"If?" Halfhyde broke in with a laugh, "*If*? Do you think your cable party won't be seen on the fo'c'sle?"

Gorsinski broke in savagely. "No, they shall not be seen, since they will not be there! Captain Chernik, you will prepare at once for sea. One man on the fo'c'sle—one man only, with a hammer, to slip the cable. This man is to keep well clear of the guns, and is not to move too quickly. He will *saunter* to his task. Until we are out of range, the bridge will not be manned. The ship will be conned from the upper deck, and steered from the after steering position in the tiller flat, with men to relay the helm orders."

"And the *Grand Duke Alexis*, Your Highness?"

"Will follow my motions. Pass the orders to her by megaphone, Captain Chernik. She is close enough and I wish no signalling by flags." Gorsinski, as the armed escort entered the cabin, gestured at Halfhyde. "Take the English officer away, and lock him in securely."

Halfhyde's heart was in his boots as the steel door of the cell was shut and locked. There was a strong possibility that Gorsinski's manoeuvre might prove successful. The outward movement would initially be slow, so slow as to be imperceptible from the shore battery; with no apparent activity along the upper decks of the ships, with the stations unmanned, there would be scant indication to Reznichenko. And if the Russian gunner's mate did spot some movement soon enough to open fire, what, in fact, would be his reaction? He had been far from anxious to slaughter comrades who might well be on his side, and for the squadron to leave the anchorage might suit his purpose well enough in any case. On the other hand, if he should open a warning or outward-speeding fire, at least a few close shaves might rattle Gorsinski's navigator into putting the *St Petersburg* hard and fast on to a sandbank! There was a touch of hope in that, but scarcely more than a touch. Once Gorsinski was clear of the anchorage, Halfhyde's threat would become as empty as a finished bottle. From then on it would be up to Captain Fitzsimmons in the *Aurora*, who would in fact have no means of knowing what the situation was, even if he should happen to make contact at all.

Sitting on the shelf-like bunk in the narrow cell, Halfhyde put his head in his hands and swore bitterly as he heard the clunk of the cable and the sound of hammering on the fo'c'sle above, the indication that the *St Petersburg* was preparing to slip, with a seaman ready to knock away the securing pin from the joining-shackle on deck so as to leave the anchor, together with a length of cable, on the bottom. Reznichenko might get some warning, perhaps, from a sudden upsurge of black smoke from the cruiser's funnels, but it was problematic that he would act on this, since Gorsinski's squadron had maintained steam continuously whilst in the anchorage, and increased smoke need not necessarily be interpreted as heralding a move to sea.

A few moments later Halfhyde felt the sudden slight whip that jerked the fore part of the cruiser as the hammer knocked out the pin and the weight of some four shackles of heavy cable was let go; then came the clatter and roar as the end of the cable flailed through the hawse-pipe, followed by a heavy splash, and then, immediately, by the shudder of the plates and decks as the thrust of the engines came on the main shaft and the propellers began churning up the mud and sand of the bottom.

Halfhyde counted away the seconds. Already the ship was moving, however slowly. He began now, to hear the hiss of water past her sides as she gathered way towards the open sea, widening the range. Then Halfhyde heard the thunderous roar from the fort, a mighty blast of sound that reached down even to the cell flat as, apparently, all four of the guns opened together. Intently, Halfhyde listened, hopeful that he might hear the splashes, the fall of shot that might with any luck panic the vessel's navigating officer into recommending more speed than was ever wise in the Bight of Benin. He heard, he fancied, one heavy splash close by the hull, and waited to hear the water-spout dropping down on to the upper deck. But this he never heard. It was lost in the terrible din, the explosion and the ripping of steel plates and the harsh roar of escaping steam that came from aft, to be followed by the cries of men and a judder that ran right through the ship.

Halfhyde was hardly conscious of the shout of triumph that came from his own lips. Reznichenko, whether by an accident of laying or by intent, seemed to have stopped Gorsinski's flagship in her tracks.

Chapter 17

PULLING at his beard, Fitzsimmons paced his cabin while the Commander waited. Fitzsimmons said, "I don't mind a fight, Commander. It's the Admiralty that worries me."

"Yes, sir."

"It's a dreadful decision to have to make."

"But inevitable."

Fitzsimmons raised an eyebrow. "You think so?"

"I do, most strongly, sir. Gunfire . . . that must mean Halfhyde's in trouble. He was under orders to reconnoitre the forts."

"Yes—reconnoitre! Not provoke them to action." The Captain continued his restless prowl. "If I enter, I may be forced to precipitate the very thing the Admiralty will most deplore. I'll be in breach of my explicit orders not to provoke a war situation, Commander! Do you not see that?"

"Yes, I see it," the Commander said shortly. "The fact still remains, and I've said this before, you can't leave Halfhyde and Runcorn to face it alone. You can't let them down, sir! If that's to happen, then I can't answer for the ship's company."

Fitzsimmons's face reddened. "What d'you mean by that, Commander?"

The Commander gave a diplomatic answer. "They've put two and two together, sir—it's natural, and can't be prevented in any warship. And they're intensely loyal and patriotic, as you know. My fear is that there may be talk when we get back to Portsmouth. That's something else the Admiralty wouldn't like "

"Talk?"

"I think you know what I mean, sir. Talk about what's supposed to be secret, talk that could reach back even to Russian ears when the newspapers pick it up. That would be very bad diplomatically—disastrous even." The Commander paused. "A British attempt to protect an area of trade and influence that failed to come off, because . . ."

"Because what, Commander—*because what?*"

The Commander shrugged. "I'm sorry sir. I was just thinking aloud. It's really not for me to say what might pass through the men's minds . . . or the Board of Admiralty's."

Glowering, Fitzsimmons sat down at his roll-top desk and stared out through a port at the grey sea waste, tapping his fingers on a blotter. The Commander knew that his Captain's thoughts were as grey, as bitter as that rising sea. As with so many captains and admirals before him, Fitzsimmons faced a possible end to his career whichever way he decided. The virtue lay as ever in success, the crime in failure.

The Commander helped Fitzsimmons out. He said on a note of reflection, "We can enter peacefully enough, sir. We're not beholden to the Russians, we need no permission from them."

"Thank you, I'm aware of that, Commander." Fitzsimmons got to his feet. "You shall have my decision shortly. For the present, we continue to the northern limit of our area, and wait."

Aboard the *St Petersburg,* the after part of the ship was a shambles of torn metal and bloodily lacerated bodies. The shell from the fort had burst on its point of impact, right on the cruiser's after gunshield, and had fragmented that gun and with it a large part of the personnel who had been on the upper deck conning the ship out to sea on Prince Gorsinski's order. The explosion of the heavy shell had also torn out the after funnel and caused consequential damage in the boiler-room, though this was in fact slight, and the cruiser was still under way and was now being steered from the bridge. Soon after the hit, Halfhyde's cell door was opened up and he was told to come out.

"Why?" he asked, laughing in the face of an officer. "Is the ship sinking, and is Prince Gorsinski anxious for my safety?"

"You are wanted on the upper deck," was all the officer would tell him. "Come quickly."

A seaman was waiting with a rifle. The muzzel was pushed against Halfhyde's back and the officer, moving ahead, led the way to the upper deck. They climbed to the navigating bridge, where waited Prince Gorsinski, who was unharmed. He was glaring back at the guns of the battery, now silent. As he swung round at the party's approach, his face was contorted and devilish. "Lieutenant Halfhyde," he said, "my navigating officer is dead, killed by the shell from the fort. You told me you had served in the Bight after you left Russia that you have special knowledge of the waters."

"True," Halfhyde said.

"Then," said Gorsinski, "you shall pilot my ships out to sea. None other of my officers, or myself, has previous experience of the Bight."

"Beware, beware the Bight of Benin," Halfhyde murmured,

his eyes gleaming, "It's worse to get out than it is to get in!" Those could be true words under certain circumstances, and Halfhyde's professional eye had noted the ebbing tide that would badly decrease the soundings for a deep-draught heavy cruiser. "What if I should put you on a mudbank, Prince Gorsinski?"

"I think you will not do that," the Russian answered, "for there will be men at your side with rifles. You will navigate literally for your life. You will have all the assistance you need —charts, leadsmen, lookouts, everything—and the *Grand Duke Alexis* will be under orders to follow closely, steering into my wake one cable's-length astern." He reached forward with the telescope he was carrying and laid its end against Halfhyde's chest. "You will be held responsible for the safety of both ships, Lieutenant Halfhyde."

Halfhyde looked out across the floating scum of the anchorage towards the fort. He was unable to pick out the guns beneath the rain-filled sky that dropped down to touch the tops of the trees themselves. Reznichenko, having scored his unexpected hit, and having seen the outward movement of the ships, would in all probability be withdrawing now. Halfhyde's concern was for Midshipman Runcorn, shivering in his fever: would the mutineers have taken him with them in their retreat to the African interior, or would Reznichenko decide he had a better chance if left within the fort? Probably the latter, Halfhyde fancied, since to carry the sick would be dangerous for all concerned. But wherever he was, Runcorn had an immediate need for medical attention. An appeal could perhaps be made to Gorsinski, but to admit the fact that Runcorn was desperately ill would confirm to Gorsinski that there was other assistance

in the fort, assistance that could only be provided by the mutineers. Whether or not Gorsinski had realized this, Halfhyde's
word to Reznichenko clearly precluded his own confirmation,
and in fact, Gorsinski was highly unlikely to jeopardize the outward movement of his squadron in order to land a doctor.

Halfhyde turned back to the Russian admiral. "If I must
pilot you out, then I shall do so," he said. "But on one condition only."

"You are in no position to make conditions, Lieutenant
Halfhyde."

"Am I not?" Halfhyde smiled coldly. "I'll admit the point that
you can kill me now if you've a mind to, but may I ask how,
in that event, you're going to take your ships to sea, Prince
Gorsinski, since you are so clearly unable to do so yourself?"

Gorsinski scowled, his face dark with anger. "Do you wish
to die now? I have only to give the order!"

"Then do so," Halfhyde said indifferently, shrugging his
shoulders. "I don't doubt that you'll contrive the death penalty
for me in Russia, so why should I prolong the agony? Can you
tell me that?"

He met the Russian's eye squarely, his lips tilting in a sardonic smile. In that moment he genuinely felt little regard for
his life. It was true enough that Russia spelled death, and it
was clear that already he had exceeded his orders from the
Admiralty to the point where once again half-pay loomed large,
if not dismissal. Thus even the possibility of another escape
from Prince Gorsinski had its blacker side.

The two men stared at each other for a full minute. Then
Gorsinski, perhaps reading an unshakable determination in
Halfhyde's face, gave way.

"What," he asked savagely, "is your condition?"

Halfhyde said, "Once your ships are out of range from the fort, I ask you to anchor again—you have more than the one anchor—and put me ashore at the jetty in the river."

"For what purpose?"

"I have unfinished business, sir."

"Indeed! Of what nature?"

"There is my midshipman."

"Who can look after himself, Lieutenant Halfhyde!"

"Well, perhaps he can," Halfhyde said, "and the better now your squadron is leaving. You may be sure that British warships will enter the Bight once word reaches London of what you are doing with the traders from Fishtown, and of what the further purposes of your government are. Nevertheless, I ask—"

"You are too wordy for a seaman, Lieutenant Halfhyde," Gorsinski interrupted. "You talk of my squadron leaving. It will not necessarily do so, once I am clear of the guns. I, too, have unfinished business in the Bight."

"May I ask what, sir?"

"Yes, you may!" Gorsinski answered harshly. "It is this, for since you are going to return to Russia with me, I shall now confirm what once you asked: I am under orders to establish a strong Russian base in Fishtown to break your sea links with Cape Town and Simon's Town whenever my government so decides."

"In other words, when you make war upon us?"

"Yes!" Gorsinski shouted in his face. "Yes, yes, yes! Now—to work, Lieutenant Halfhyde, and remember, your life will be worth nothing if my ships are put in hazard!"

Gorsinski called up three armed seamen, who closed in on

Halfhyde. As the great shore battery remained silent, the *St Petersburg* drifted slowly ahead and off her starboard quarter, the *Grand Duke Alexis*, in response a few moments later to a flag hoist from the signal mast of the *St Petersburg*, headed towards the Admiral to take station close astern.

"Keep your engines at dead slow," Halfhyde said, bending to the azimuth circle on the standard compass. Quickly he took his bearings on two of Fishtown's leading-marks, obtaining a fix, then plotted the ship's exact position on the chart, noting the proximity of the mudbanks, which, as he knew from experience, were liable to shift and thus give the lie to the chart's information. "Port ten . . . Midships, steady." "Steady," the quartermaster reported as he brought the wheel over to meet the swing. Then: "Course, two hundred and sixty-seven degrees."

Halfhyde nodded, ears alert for the reports from the men in the chains as they swung their leads. Walking to the side of the bridge, he stared down into the grey-brown water, unable, because of the floating muck, to deduce from the look of the surface what might lie beneath. Behind him, watching every movement, came the men with the rifles. Halfhyde scowled blackly. The presence of armed threat scarcely helped a proper concentration on safe pilotage in such tricky waters—tricky chiefly, it was true, for ships attempting to come out across the sand bar, yet tricky enough even in the anchorage for steam warships of the length, beam and draft of the *St Petersburg*. Nor did Gorsinski decrease the fast-building tension as the cruiser nosed out from the anchorage. He, too, kept close to Halfhyde, exuding an irritating if silent criticism.

"Steer two degrees to port," Halfhyde ordered.

"Two degrees to port." Slowly, carefully, the helm was put

over. "Course, two hundred and sixty-six degrees."

"Steady as you go." Halfhyde looked down again into the water. There was, by the chart, a long bank of mud on the starboard side. A few moments later, the leadsman in the starboard chains reported a sharp decrease in the soundings on that side and Halfhyde brought the ship round another two degrees to port and waited for the leadsman to sing out again. The next report indicated a little more water to starboard. Steady on her course, the *St Petersburg* moved on; then the rain started, a sheeting downpour that enclosed the vessel in a surrounding wall of water so that all sight of the shore was lost and the great bulk of the *Grand Duke Alexis,* so close astern, faded totally into the cloudburst that seemed to join sea to sky.

At once Gorsinski ordered the main engines stopped and the steam siren sounded in warning to the *Grand Duke Alexis.* In the teeming rain they drifted, silently, a dead ship. For some fifteen minutes the rain-blindness continued, then the downpour eased a little, restoring enough visibility for movement. As the shape of the *Grand Duke Alexis* loomed blackly through the rain, Gorsinski ordered a fog buoy to be streamed and once again the engines beat into life. They moved slowly on, the ship astern nosing her stem up to the fog buoy on the end of its line, Gorsinski conferred with his Flag Captain. This was no place to anchor: the first swing would carry their stern and their propellors on to the mud.

"As soon as there's enough clear water all round, I shall anchor," Gorsinsinki said. "After that, we shall retake the fort. Lieutenant Halfhyde?"

"Yes, sir?"

"How much farther, to clear water?"

Halfhyde glanced at the chart and made a quick, dead-reckoning calculation from his last fix. "Two miles, give or take a little."

Gorsinski grunted. "Make it in safety, Lieutenant—" He broke off sharply as a loud cry came from the lookout right forward in the eyes of the ship. It was an indistinct cry, but Gorsinski, understandably perhaps, took it as a warning of mudbanks ahead beneath the scum on the ebb tide. He himself ran for the engine-room telegraphs and drew the handles back—right over twice, signalling Emergency Full Astern. Bells rang, were repeated back, and the St Petersburg shuddered throughout her length as the engines began their thrash astern to pull her up in her tracks before her stem embedded. As her way checked, there was another shout from the fo'c'sle-head "Sir, she is on the port bow, and closing!"

"A ship, by the great God!" Gorsinski, his face white, lifted his telescope, peering through the rain. As he did so, Halfhyde saw the emerging shape, the lean grey cruiser coming out of the rain's misting cloak with the White Ensign flying from the jackstaff.

Chapter 18

THE sudden appearance of British power, with he knew not how many more ships out of his sight behind, seemed to paralyze Prince Gorsinski. He remained staring, open-mouthed; and he remained inactive a shade too long. Just as the Flag Captain himself, without waiting for orders from his Admiral, pulled over the engine room telegraph handles, the *St Petersburg*, with sternway still upon her, took the mud aft, her thrashing propellors biting in deep before they jammed the main shafts solid. The cruiser stopped dead, quivering and lurching, victim of a grinding jolt that everywhere threw men flat on the decks, two of the personnel on the navigating bridge being projected beneath the forward guard-rail to crash on the upper deck below. Halfhyde, shot off his feet with the rest, fetched up against a stanchion. Pulling himself quickly to his feet, he ran for the starboard rail of the navigating bridge and was over the side before Gorsinski or the men with the rifles had collected themselves.

Diving, Halfhyde went deep into water clouded by the churned-up scum and mud. When he surfaced well clear of the *St Petersburg's* imprisoned hull, he was not spotted at once. But a few moments later his head was seen rising from the filth, and rifle fire started from the Russian ship's fo'c'sle and navigating bridge. Bullets spattered around Halfhyde, and once again, after taking a deep lungful of air, he went down, swimming strongly.

When next he came to the surface, he was no more than a cable's length from the *Aurora*. A shout went up when he was seen. He waved. He called out, "It's me, Halfhyde. Send down a rope's end." He swam towards the ship's side, making for a point below the bridge, where a party of seamen were mustered under a petty officer. As he approached, a rope snaked down, dangling into the water. Halfhyde reached it and held fast. "Heave away!" he shouted to the petty officer. Within half a minute, he was dripping water and stinking scum on the fo'c'sle, to be joined by Captain Fitzsimmons who had hurried down from the bridge, having already sent a messenger for the Fleet Surgeon.

"Mr Halfhyde, what shape are you in?"

"Fair enough, sir."

"Then your report quickly, if you please. Why were you fired upon by the Russians?"

"They didn't want me to get away," Halfhyde said patiently, with a glimmer of amusement in his eyes. "Prince Gorsinski is a very angry man, especially as his flagship's hard aground aft and almost certainly won't come off again, at least not without the assistance of some powerful tugs from Sevastopol before the swell breaks her up!"

"And Mr Runcorn?" Fitzsimmons's beard jutted, head forward as he stood with feet apart and hands behind his back. "Where is Mr Runcorn?"

"Sick with malaria, sir, inside the fort behind the town— and in need of medical attention. But the most pressing matter, sir, is that there are British subjects held aboard the *Grand Duke*

Alexis." In as few words as possible, Halfhyde put his captain in possession of all the essential facts. "I submit, sir, that the Russians have already committed an act close enough—"

"To an act of war, Mr Halfhyde?"

Halfhyde nodded. "A hostile act, sir, that gives you the right to board and demand—"

"I shall be the judge of my own actions, Mr Halfhyde!" Fitzsimmons broke in coldly. He turned away, his face sombre, rain cascading from the gleaming black oilskin and sou'wester. He stared across the muddy water towards the Russian flagship, which, clearly seen now, had veered across the channel and seemed to be held by the bows as well as by the stern. All at once Fitzsimmons gave a sharp exclamation and pointed wordlessly towards the *St Petersburg.* Following the Captain's pointing finger, Halfhyde gave a shout of laughter. The *Grand Duke Alexis,* evidently not quick enough to check her way when the flagship's engines had been put astern, had smashed into the port side of the flagship towards her after end, embedding deep into the plates for some ten to fifteen feet. There was a roar of steam from burst pipes below, and the cries of men could be heard clear across the rain-slashed water.

"By God!" Fitzsimmons said, staring. "She'll be in a fair mess aft, Mr Halfhyde, and taking water fast, I'll be bound!"

"True, sir. And her main shafts in a worse way than ever. Neither ship can survive this, sir, not in the ground-swell of the Bight. His Highness'll not leave until the Imperial Navy comes to fetch him out!"

"Then we shall not need to be precipitate, Mr Halfhyde."

"Sir?"

"I shall not *storm* Prince Gorsinski with boarding parties

armed to the teeth, Mr Halfhyde," Fitzsimmons said in a lofty tone, "I shall *ask permission* to board, in a spirit of friendship, and with offers of help. I think I can do no less."

Halfhyde said coldly, "Do you indeed, sir."

"I do—in the first instance at any rate."

"I shall go with you, sir."

"No, you will not." Fitzsimmons lifted a hand. "The Commander will accompany me, while you make your way ashore and retrieve Mr Runcorn from his fort. You need have no fear. I shall bear in mind all you have told me, and I note that the Russian mutineers gave vital assistance."

"And I gave my word as a British officer that they would never be let down, sir."

Fitzsimmons nodded. "Noted, Mr Halfhyde. Commander?"

"Sir?"

"Call away all boats, if you please, and swing out the quarter and lower booms. Muster armed parties of seamen and marines, the former to stand by should I require them to be sent to the Russian flagship, the latter to embark in cutters and make the passage of the sand bar under Mr Halfhyde's pilotage. Their orders are to take over the shore battery and remain there. Other of the ship's boats are to lie off to seaward of the surf and act as rescue craft if the marines should be spilled out. In the meantime, the ship is to go to action stations, but quietly, with no bugles or alarm bells sounding. All guns that can do so will be brought to bear on the Russian ships. My hope is that I shall not need to use them. The British Government has no desire for war. Understood, Commander?"

"Yes, sir."

"Then see to it, if you please, at once. Chief Yeoman of Signals?"

"Sir?"

"Make a signal to Admiral Prince Gorsinski. I request permission to come aboard."

"Aye, aye, sir."

"Fleet Surgeon, Mr Runcorn is sick ashore. Since you will be needed here, or may be, kindly send your Assistant Surgeon to accompany Mr Halfhyde with the necessary medicines to attack malaria."

"Sir, a diagnosis has not—"

"That is your affair, Fleet Surgeon. I know nothing of medicine, but malaria appears to be indicated. Mr Halfhyde, you have done well and I am pleased." All necessary orders given and commendations made, Captain Fitzsimmons, tugging at his beard, proceeded aft, speeded by a battery of salutes, to attire himself in frock coat and sword the better to wait peacefully upon the Russian aristocracy.

"How are you, Wart?"

Halfhyde, muddied again from the trek up to the battery from Fishtown and from his boat-borne progress through the muck-filled surf, bent over the midshipman, together with the Aurora's junior doctor. "By God, you've been sweating buckets, haven't you?"

"I'm better now, sir." The voice was painfully weak, little more than a whisper. Halfhyde met the doctor's eye. There was a head-shake, a sombre look; but there were things Halfhyde had to know.

"Wart, the mutineers. Reznichenko. They've gone. When did they go?"

It was an obvious effort but the wart made it. "They left after the *Aurora* was seen to enter, sir. After the hit on the flagship they stayed by the guns, ready to fire on any ship's boats sent by Prince Gorsinski."

Halfhyde touched a glass by the wart's bed. "They left medicine, I see—quinine. They were good fellows."

He straightened with a sigh. Reznichenko had also seen to it that Runcorn was warmly tucked into bed with all available blankets, though the wart's feverish tossing had in fact dislodged most of them. Halfhyde, catching the doctor's eye, moved with him away from the bed. In the doorway he asked, "Well, doctor? What d'you think?"

"He'd have died if we hadn't come, that's certain. But now . . ."

"Yes?" Halfhyde's voice was sharp.

"It's hard to say. I think he'll pull through. He's young and otherwise fit. I believe he'll respond."

"You'll not risk him through the surf, will you?"

"No," the Assistant Surgeon said. "I shall look after him where he is till he's fit to make the passage back to the ship."

Gorsinski shook a fist in the very face of Captain Fitzsimmons, who remained calm and aloof, reading an awareness of defeat into the Russian's raging. "You exceed the wishes of your government!" Gorsinski stormed.

"As you do of yours," Fitzsimmons said indifferently. "On that point, it's stalemate. Not on others, however."

"You—"

Fitzsimmons lifted a hand, and smiled coldly. "Your Highness, listen, if you please. You have lost one ship; you have stranded two. You have served yourself as badly as my officers have served me well. *You are in no position to lay down the law.* I repeat: all the Fishtown traders will be released at once, and put ashore to resume their normal business—"

"No!" Gorsinski shook both fists in the air. *"No, no, no!"*

"Then," Fitzsimmons said, bringing out a white linen handkerchief to dust specks from his immaculate uniform, "you will consider your ships and yourself to be under arrest."

"Arrest, fiddlesticks!"

"On the contrary, Your Highness. This is a wholly enforceable arrest."

"Your one piddling ship?"

"Ah," Fitzsimmons said, wagging a finger in the Russian's face, "my one piddling ship is manoeuvrable! Yours are not. Yours are stuck fast in the mud and in each other, which betrays most poor qualities of pilotage and ship-handling. And may I remind you that the shore battery will by now be under my orders." He paused. "You must now talk sense, Prince Gorsinski, for I tell you one thing more. Whilst cruising outside the Gulf to await Mr Halfhyde and Mr Runcorn, I was given intelligence by one of our cruisers on passage to the Cape—intelligence from Gibraltar that a British battle squadron is steaming south to lie off the Bight, together with a light-cruiser squadron that will enter the Bight itself." Fitzsimmons got to his feet, large and formidable, and as autocratic as Gorsinski himself. "You see, word of your coming has reached the Admiralty, but word of your own mishaps is unlikely to reach your own high command, as you must realize. The

Russian attempt to create a sphere of influence in West Africa has failed. The British Navy will not, in future, neglect this station, Your Highness! In the meantime I must ask you not to attempt to land men at the jetty."

"Damn you, Captain, for your impertinence! Do you not understand, I have mutineers to be arrested!"

"Indeed." Fitzsimmons gave an ironic bow. "That is your concern, not mine. You will not be permitted landing-parties. Good day to you, Your Highness. I'll be obliged if you'll kindly have my galley called alongside."

"Young Runcorn," the Fleet Surgeon said, three days later, coming into the wardroom where Halfhyde was sitting with a glass of whisky in his hand. "You can cut along and see him if you like."

"Thank you, Doctor." Halfhyde got to his feet. "How is he?"

"Better. Very much on the mend."

"The Lord be praised! I'd hate to face a sorrowing mother." Halfhyde left the wardroom and made his way along the alleyways towards the sick bay, where the wart was lying in a cot suspended from the deckhead, looking washed out but clear-eyed and relaxed. Smiling, Halfhyde sat by the cot and nodded dismissingly at the sick-berth attendant, who left them alone behind a curtain drawn between the midshipman and the ratings' sick quarters. "Well done, Wart."

"Sir?" The eyes were questioning.

"Oh, I meant well done to pull through so nicely. But it goes for other things too, Wart. As a matter of fact, you did *damn* well. Proud to have served with you, Mr Midshipman Runcorn!" Rising briefly, Halfhyde gave a mock bow, but his face and the smile on it were wholly sincere. "Now you're *compos mentis,* you'll want to hear how the matter ended, I don't doubt."

"Has it ended, sir?"

"So far as the *Aurora's* concerned, it has. The objectives have been achieved, and the traders have been put ashore. Oh, I've no doubt the diplomatic reverberations will continue for some quite considerable time, but militarily, as it were, the Captain did very well." In full detail, Halfhyde gave Runcorn the story as told him by Fitzsimmons. "It was fifty percent bluff, I suppose, but Gorsinski was too shaken by being fast in the Benin mud, and by having simmering mutiny below decks, to do anything but cave in. No more risks for His Highness! It wasn't bluff about the arrival of the battle squadron and the light cruisers, though. They're expected daily."

"How about Reznichenko, sir?"

Halfhyde laughed. "Clear away! The Captain's had boats patrolling round the Russians and not a man's been allowed ashore either by native canoe or across the bar in the boats. Reznichenko'll be as all right as *we* could make it. We've kept our word, Wart, kept faith."

"I'm glad, sir." Runcorn paused, looking introspective. "And us, sir? What are your orders, sir?"

"Orders for home," Halfhyde said with a curious tinge of regret that, for him, home meant waiting upon the Board of Admiralty in the first instance, to have his recent activities weighed and his fitness for future employment duly considered. Which way the balance went would depend very largely on the diplomatic dust-storm and how much of that disturbed dust fell upon the heads of the members of the Board themselves. Halfhyde knew he had not shirked his duty, and that was something. Yet, in grossly exceeding that duty, he could not but be aware that havoc caused to an officially friendly Power, plus an initial unprovoked attack upon a lieutenant of that Power's naval service, plus the slaughter of the soldiers of the gun battery, plus active encouragement of mutineers, might well cause misgivings in high places. Indeed, Fitzsimmons, who as his commanding officer could not escape all censure and knew it, had already had harsh words to say. Fitzsimmons apart, however, all that was for the future,

Halfhyde repeated, "Orders for home, Mr Runcorn. We sail upon the arrival of the light cruisers, for Portsmouth, home, and beauty." He got up. "Sleep now, Wart. Get your strength up. Good night."

"Good night, sir."

Halfhyde left the sick bay and climbed to the upper deck. He looked out at the shore as the watery sky lost its light, looked across at the Russian cruisers, lying as dead ships across the fairway, one down by the stern, the other by the bow, with collision mats draped over the gaping plates like hairy curtains. As he watched, a bugle sounded the Still from the *Aurora's* quarterdeck; then the strains of Sunset broke the silence of the Bight. Right aft, a signalman slowly lowered the White Ensign: it was the end of one more day of a lately somewhat disturbed naval routine. The Carry On sounded and Halfhyde went below to dinner in the wardroom, thinking his own thoughts.

Seven days later, by which time Halfhyde had taken his leave of old friends ashore, a winking masthead light out in the Gulf of Guinea heralded the arrival of the light-cruiser squadron, and the following morning, upon being officially relieved of his watching brief, Captain Fitzsimmons took the *Aurora* out to sea, with Halfhyde conning the ship. Leaving behind them the forlorn remains of the *Romanov*, settled into the mud in three seperate sections, with her broken superstructure and fighting top already rusting into dereliction, they steamed past the locked-together remainder of the Russian squadron. Salutes were formally exchanged by bugle—Fitzsimmons stuck to the niceties. He made a final signal: ADMIRAL PRINCE GORSINSKI FROM AURORA. I SHALL REPORT YOUR PLIGHT TO REAR-ADMIRAL GIBRALTAR FOR ONWARD TRANSMISSION TO THE COURT OF ST PETERSBURG. Then they swept grandly outwards, belching black smoke over the Russians, with a rain-swept band of the Royal Marine Light Infantry beating out "Rule, Britannia."

There was a lump in Halfhyde's throat as he heard the sounding brass and its boastful pomp. "Rule, Britannia" . . . boastful, yes, but for so long as the British Fleet was in being to command the seven seas, it was true and substantial.